"He's coming!"

Sierra turned in her seat.

"Let's get out of here." Cole flipped on the SUV's flashing red-and-blue lights and sped toward Sedona. And so did the car in the distance.

Cole's knuckles turned white as he gripped the steering wheel.

"What can I do?" Sierra leaned closer to the front seat. "Should I call 911?"

"The chief is sending help." Cole caught a glimpse of Shaw pulling up next to the police cruiser. A shot rang out, and Thomas's passenger window exploded. The officer swerved onto the shoulder before veering back onto the road.

Shaw slowed just enough to get a better aim at the cruiser and shot out a back tire. Officer Thomas kept driving. More shots followed, and the cruiser flipped.

"No!" Sierra screamed. Danny cried out.

"Get down! And stay there." More cars pulled over as they raced down the road. Hopefully, someone would call 911 to report the rollover.

Through the rearview mirror, he could see Sierra folded over the car seat, shielding Danny with her body.

Tina Wheeler is a retired teacher and award-winning author. She enjoys spending time with her large extended family, brainstorming with writing friends, discovering new restaurants and traveling with her husband. Although she grew up near a desert in Arizona, her favorite place to plot a new story is on a balcony overlooking the ocean.

Books by Tina Wheeler

Love Inspired Suspense

Ranch Under Fire
Ranch Showdown

Visit the Author Profile page at LoveInspired.com.

RANCH SHOWDOWN

TINA WHEELER

LOVE INSPIRED SUSPENSE
INSPIRATIONAL ROMANCE

LOVE INSPIRED® SUSPENSE
INSPIRATIONAL ROMANCE

Recycling programs
for this product may
not exist in your area.

ISBN-13: 978-1-335-59899-8

Ranch Showdown

Love Inspired
22 Adelaide St. West, 41st Floor
Toronto, Ontario M5H 4E3, Canada
www.LoveInspired.com

Printed in U.S.A.

Be strong and of a good courage, fear not, nor be afraid of them: for the Lord thy God, he it is that doth go with thee; he will not fail thee, nor forsake thee.

—*Deuteronomy* 31:6

To my writing friends who guide and encourage me, especially Kathryne Kennedy, the Savvy Scribes and Sassy Storytellers.

ONE

Some mornings felt like entire days, and this was one of them. With a sigh, Sierra Lowery turned the key in her SUV's ignition, shutting the engine off. She waited for the sense of comfort that usually flowed over her after returning home from a stressful photo shoot, but today peace eluded her. In its place was the disturbing feeling that something wasn't right. Unable to put her finger on it, she slipped out of the driver's seat and rounded her vehicle to open the back end.

She reached inside for the case containing her camera, wallet and phone. After shrugging the strap over her shoulder, she grabbed hold of the nylon bag protecting her tripod. Although her client had been more than demanding on this chilly January morning, Sierra had to admit that the shots of the bride-to-be in front of Sedona's Cathedral Rock were among the best she'd taken since establishing her business in Arizona eleven years ago.

The box of diapers and formula shoved to the side would have to wait until after she hauled in this load. Once everything was inside, she'd walk the short distance next door to collect her precious three-month-old nephew, Danny, from the babysitter. Thinking of him brought on a smile. A few days ago, she hadn't known he existed, and now she was watching over him while her sister, Megan, flew to New Orleans. Sierra's heart grew heavy. That trip was as far from being a vacation as one could get.

After unlocking the front door of the ranch-style house where she and her sister had grown up, she carried her bags inside the living room and recognized the scent of coffee. Was Megan back already? She hadn't mentioned a change of plans when they spoke over the phone the previous morning.

Sierra's gaze fell on the end table—someone had opened the drawer. She turned and spotted the cushions of the gray-colored sofa in disarray and the stuffing of the throw pillows littering the coffee table and floor. Her pulse hitched as realization struck. She glanced about at her ransacked home, listening for any sign an intruder might still be there.

"Shut the door." A man she didn't know strolled out of her kitchen, sporting black-framed glasses, a graying goatee and surgical gloves. He held a gun in one hand and a ceramic mug in the other. That had to be the coffee she smelled. He took a sip before placing the mug on the dining room table next to a teddy bear she'd never seen before.

Sierra froze, still gripping the bags she'd carried inside. Her eyes widened, and her heart thundered in her chest as she realized who stood before her. *Oliver Vogel.* Her sister's ex-boyfriend. Megan had said his first name didn't fit him when she'd described him in great detail—with *deadly* topping the list.

"Do as I say, or I'll go to your neighbor's house, kill everyone inside and take my son. Your sister will *never* see him again." His warning had her stumbling backward.

Vogel leaned against the wooden table and picked up the teddy bear by its neck. His expression twisted into a menacing glare as he squeezed the toy with his large hand. The gun's aim never shifted away from her.

Sierra's mind clouded, and her knees threatened to buckle. She would do whatever it took to prevent this monster from taking her nephew. If she had to die to fulfill the promise she'd made to Megan to keep the baby safe, so be it.

Shut the door. His demand repeated in her head.

Unable to speak, Sierra turned, and the bags she was holding bounced against her sides. She let them fall to the hardwood floor before slowly reaching for the knob with a trembling hand.

Maybe someone would walk by, and she could signal for help. But as she pressed the door into its frame, the only movement outside came from leaves swept down the residential street by a gust of wind.

"Secure the bolt!"

Sierra jerked in reaction to his anger, then followed his command, locking out help—and hope. She sucked in a shuddering breath and turned to face the madman, unsure what he wanted and too afraid to ask.

Vogel wasn't supposed to be here. When Megan had left him in Yuma a week ago, he said she couldn't make it on her own and would come running back to him.

"Where are they?" he demanded.

They? Megan and Danny? He already knew the baby was next door.

"Don't act like you don't know what I'm talking about. The papers! Where are they?"

Sierra's stomach clenched. Megan would never have willingly told him about the copies she'd made of his ledger and fake IDs. "Where's my sister? What did you do to her?"

"Don't worry. You'll see your traitorous sister again—*if* I get what I want," Vogel sneered as he pushed away from the table, taking slow, deliberate steps toward Sierra. "My contacts in New Orleans say Megan's been trying to peddle evidence against me."

Megan wasn't peddling anything. She was trying to find someone she could trust to put Vogel away for murder.

"What you want isn't here." Sierra needed a weapon. She took one hesitant step toward the wooden bookcase, then another, until she bumped into a shelf. Her mystery novels slid off and onto the floor with a thud. Remembering the heavy paperweight she'd used as a bookend, she glanced at her feet. It wasn't there. She didn't dare turn to look for it with him watching her every move.

"I heard your sister hid the papers here to keep them from falling into the wrong hands." He chuckled before narrowing his dark eyes. "As if she could keep me from getting anything I want."

His sinister tone wasn't an act; the man was pure evil. How he had managed to fool Megan for so long was a wonder. Although her sister had a thing for bad boys, she'd managed to avoid hardened criminals. Until two years ago, when she'd met Vogel in a bar.

"Then someone lied to you," Sierra protested. "They're not here."

A guttural roar erupted from Vogel like a

fiery volcano. He swung out, slamming his fist into a lamp, sending it smashing into a wall.

Sierra jumped back, knocking into the bookcase again. She turned, located the paperweight at the far end of the shelf, grabbed it and hurled it at his head. He lifted his hands to protect his face, and the gun fired into the wall.

She ran for the door, but he lunged on top of her, and they fell forward onto the floor. Her elbows hit hard, and pain shot up her arms.

"You little…" He gripped her tighter, and the stench of stale cigarettes mixed with coffee made her gag.

Loud pounding yanked their attention to the front door.

"Sierra! Are you okay?" The concerned voice belonged to her neighbor, Hank Anderson. His teenage daughter was watching Danny.

Sierra feared they might all be outside together. *Surely he wouldn't bring them along after hearing a gunshot.*

"Call the police!" she yelled before Vogel gripped her throat with his gloved fingers and squeezed.

"I'll be right back!" Hank promised.

Vogel whispered into her ear, "You're dead."

With her windpipe threatening to collapse, she struggled to shake him off. To breathe. The teddy bear, barely out of reach at the foot of the sofa, reminded her of Danny and why she had to remain strong. Why she had to fight. "Pa... pers," she managed to force out.

"What was that?" He loosened his grip.

"I'll find them." She coughed and sucked air into her burning lungs. "I need time."

He grabbed a clump of her hair and pulled her head back toward him. "You have forty-eight hours. And if you even think of giving those papers to the cops—"

"I won't. I promise." She stared at the ceiling as he gripped her hair tighter. "I'll leave a comment on my photography blog when I find them," she blurted out, worried he might change his mind and shoot her.

Pounding on the door resumed. "Sierra! The police are coming."

"If I don't get those papers, I'll kill you and take my son. He'll grow up to be just like me." Sirens blared in the distance. Vogel suddenly released his grip and removed his weight from Sierra's back. His parting gift was a swift kick to her upper arm. "You have forty-eight hours," he reminded her before escaping through the dining room's sliding glass door.

Each cough brought on more aches and pain. Her body would be one massive bruise from head to toe by tomorrow morning.

A large rock broke through the front window and blinds before skidding across the coffee table. "Sierra!" her neighbor yelled into the opening. "Answer me!"

"I'm coming." She tried to ignore her throbbing arm while pushing against the sofa to stand. Tears welled in her eyes, blurring her vision as she tugged open the door and gazed over at the familiar face. "I'm okay," she claimed on another cough.

Hank, a middle-aged grocery store manager, took one look at her and surmised, "No, you're not. What happened here?" With one arm wrapped around her back, he escorted her out front as police cruisers pulled up to the curb.

She ignored his question and asked one of her own. "Where's Danny?"

"He's with Chelsea," he answered, just as his wife stepped outside, holding a yellow baby blanket—but no baby. Ellen Anderson stared at them with wide eyes.

Panic ripped through Sierra. Did Vogel go next door to take his son? To ensure he got the papers? "Danny!"

Sierra evaded the officers crossing the lawn as she rushed toward Ellen, leaving Hank to deal with the police.

An SUV stopped behind the cruisers, and a tall cowboy—a walking memory from her past—pushed open the driver's door and stepped out.

Not now. No one, not even Detective Cole Walker, would distract her from going to her nephew right this minute.

It had been twelve years since Cole had spoken to his former college girlfriend. He'd seen Sierra Lowery from afar at restaurants or grocery stores, even at a wedding once, but he never dreamed their next conversation would come after a *shots fired* report. The dispatcher, a mutual friend, had recognized the address and notified him immediately after sending help.

The responding officers spoke briefly to the middle-aged man who had been standing with Sierra and then descended on the house, weapons ready. Meanwhile, Cole strode down the neighbor's concrete path.

"Danny!" Sierra demanded as soon as she reached a middle-aged woman who tightly gripped a yellow baby blanket. "Where's Danny?"

"Chelsea has him." The woman gestured toward the front door, where a teenage girl stood, holding an infant dressed in a blue onesie. "He's fine, Sierra. What happened? We heard a gunshot."

Curious, Cole paused and watched. The last he'd heard, Sierra was still single, living alone in the home she and her older sister had inherited from their parents. The girls had been close as children but grew apart as young adults after constant arguing. A decade ago, the sister ran off to the desert city of Yuma with a group of petty criminals.

The *shots fired* call would have made more sense if Megan still lived in Sedona. Not now. And where did the little boy play into all this?

Sierra ran over to the teen and grabbed hold of the baby. She sobbed as she held him close, rocking him back and forth and burying her face into his shoulder. He fussed in response but quickly quieted after she patted his back and whispered in his ear.

Cole drew closer. It was apparent from her disheveled appearance that she'd been through an ordeal. "Sierra." The concern in his calm voice was genuine. It didn't matter that she'd dumped him just as he was about to propose a dozen years ago. Part of him would always care for her. But he knew better than to get emotionally involved again. "I'm a detective—"

"I heard." She lifted her face away from the baby to peer over at him.

He studied the marks on her neck. "Let's get you checked out by an EMT."

"No." She shook her head vehemently. "What we need is protection." Tears flowed freely from her red-rimmed eyes. "This is my nephew,

Danny, and we're in danger. Megan's old boyfriend has a gun. His name is Oliver Vogel. He
ran out the back door when we heard sirens,
but he'll be back." She drew in a breath, then
forged ahead as if someone might try to stop
her. "I have forty-eight hours to give him papers
I don't have, or he'll kill me and take the baby.
He's been watching us. He knows our routines
and that Danny was over here at my neighbors'
house."

The other woman gasped and pulled the teenage girl close.

Cole scanned their surroundings. Nothing
caught his eye, but this Vogel character could
be hiding nearby. "Was he alone?"

Sierra nodded; then, the average-looking middle-aged man who had been speaking to the officers joined them, and Cole introduced himself.

"I'm Hank Anderson. This is my wife, Ellen,
and our daughter, Chelsea. We've known Sierra for years." He placed his arms around his
family, huddling them together, and a gust of
wind brought on a sudden chill. "Why don't
you bring Sierra and the baby inside our home,
where it's warm."

"First, let me make sure it's safe. The suspect
could have gained access to your home while
you were out front." They readily agreed, and
Cole called over a uniformed officer for assis-

tance. He asked Sierra to provide a description of Vogel and his weapon before beginning a search of the property.

While the officer radioed in an update, Sierra turned to her neighbors. "I should leave." Her tone conveyed both fear and regret. "I'm so sorry, Hank, Ellen, Chelsea... I may have put you in danger. Megan promised he wouldn't come here. And he wouldn't have if—" Sobs prevented her from finishing her thought.

Memories of Sierra helping at church functions flashed through Cole's mind. Although time had passed, and her face was now slimmer and more angular, her belief in doing right by others appeared steadfast.

"This isn't your fault." Mr. Anderson's brow furrowed as he watched two officers, firearms drawn, enter his house. "We know you have a pure heart, Sierra."

While the older couple exchanged worried looks, Cole moved the group away from the door and asked the family, "Did you see anyone who looked out of place?"

They shook their heads. "We heard a gunshot," Mr. Anderson announced. "I saw Sierra's car and ran next door to check on her. I thought the sound might have come from there, but I wasn't sure."

Cole spent the next few minutes listening to

a recount of everything the Anderson family had heard and seen while he kept a watchful eye out for trouble.

The patrol officers soon stepped outside the front door and separated. While one spoke over the radio, the other headed toward Cole, then stated, "Both houses are clear, but Miss Lowery's was tossed."

No doubt in search of the papers Sierra had mentioned. "Finish securing the crime scene. I'll be over after I get their statements."

The officer glanced at Sierra and the baby before adding, "I'll let you know if the cruisers patrolling the area find anything."

Cole nodded in response, then ushered the group inside, out of the chilly weather. Mrs. Anderson attempted to send the teen to her room, but her husband wanted their daughter where he could see her.

Even though the premises had been searched, Cole walked over to the sliding glass door and peered out for his own peace of mind. Vogel might have jumped the stone wall between the yards during his escape. Next to a lush green lawn and flower bed, patio furniture and a grill sat on pavers. His gaze then traveled to a small garden shed with a side compartment for storing cut firewood. If anyone was crouching behind the structure, a shadow would have given him away.

Cole returned to the group, and they all took seats in the warm living room decorated in earth tones, with the teen sitting between her parents on the sofa.

Sierra sat with the baby in a wingback chair, appearing stiff and uncomfortable. She explained what had happened after returning home from her photo shoot, including odd irregularities such as smelling coffee and finding a toy bear, before she described Vogel's attack. "He claimed Megan hid copies of his ledger here in Sedona, but I know she planned to hand them over to the proper authorities in New Orleans."

Cole turned a page of his notebook. "Tell me more about this ledger."

"When Megan lived in Yuma, she almost walked in on her boyfriend's secret meeting with his good friend from out of state. Some guy Vogel met years ago through someone in his militia group. Megan hid near the garage door so they wouldn't catch her eavesdropping."

The teen's eyes had grown wide at the word *militia*, and her mother patted her jean-clad knee reassuringly.

Sierra's gaze dropped to the carpeted floor. "The other man, nicknamed Gator, handed over a stack of bills and thanked Vogel for his help with a bomb. Gator then asked if he was sure he didn't want to plant this one like he usually does, and Vogel said the target was too hot. The man said he understood and promised to pay the other half once the *hag* got what was coming to her."

Mrs. Anderson's face paled, and she reached for her husband's hand.

Sierra glanced in their direction while lifting the baby to her shoulder, most likely seeking the solace his innocence provided. Her nephew rested his head against her shoulder and closed his eyes.

Cole read the faces in the room. They had every right to be fearful. Focusing back on Sierra, he asked, "Does Megan know Gator's real name?"

"No." Sierra shook her head. "Later, Vogel wrote in a ledger, then stuffed it and the cash in a hole in the wall hidden behind a cabinet. Megan waited until he left for one of his militia meetings to snoop and discovered fake driver's licenses and passports with his picture on them. In his ledger, he kept track of dates, names, places, dollar amounts and bank account numbers alongside the fake name he used to deposit each amount. The last notation listed Gator, plus another name, fifteen thousand dollars, New Orleans and the words *construction supplies*."

Cole glanced up from his notes. "*Construction supplies* must be his code for *bomb*. It gives him plausible deniability if they're caught. He could claim he was told Gator wanted to blow up a huge tree trunk or a wall of boulders."

Sierra pressed her lips together, then kissed the baby's cheek—a sweet gesture in stark contrast to the disturbing details she'd shared. "Megan made copies of everything on one of those multipurpose printers. Then she packed bags for her and Danny and left. Vogel later sent her a text telling her he didn't know what he'd done wrong this time, but he knew she would come crawling back to him."

"And the baby?" Cole asked, noticing he had blond curls like Sierra and Megan. "Is Vogel the father?"

Sierra ran her hand over her nephew's back and touched his head with her own. "Megan said he is, but she left important papers with me, including Danny's birth certificate. It says *Father Unknown*. When I asked, she said they had broken up a week before Danny was born, and she didn't want Vogel to have any claim to him."

Sierra drew in a shaky breath. "Megan wasn't thinking straight when she went back to him. Apparently, that was a pattern that kept repeating."

"You should talk to a lawyer," Mrs. Anderson suggested in a kind, motherly tone, despite the fact that she was obviously upset a dangerous man had been next door only minutes earlier. "I don't think he can take the baby. He'd need a paternity test to prove he's the father in a court of law. He won't do that. Not with the police looking for him."

Sierra's grim expression never faltered. Not even for a second. "He doesn't care about the law. From what Gator said, Megan believes Vogel's a murderer. She remembers him being out of town on those other dates listed in his ledger."

Cole clenched his teeth before asking, "Did Megan share any other specific information she found in this ledger? Names? Places?"

"She showed it to me before she left town. Two cities listed are in South America." Sierra hesitated, her expression pensive. "I'm sorry, I can't recall anything else right now. I'll tell you if something comes back to me when my mind clears."

"Please do." Cole was still having difficulty wrapping his brain around the fact that Sierra had landed in such a volatile situation. She'd always strived for peace and routine, especially after losing her parents in a car accident twelve years ago, right after her favorite grandmother had passed away. They had a great-aunt in Arkansas, but neither sister had seen her in years.

Not much later, Sierra had told him she couldn't bear to lose anyone else she loved. And because law enforcement was a dangerous profession, she'd broken up with him. It was the same day he'd started the police academy.

Cole finished his interviews with a suggestion that the Andersons stay somewhere else for a few days. Vogel would come back for the papers. If he couldn't find Sierra at home, he might look for the baby here. He knew they babysat for her.

Hank turned to his wife. "How about a trip to California? You've been wanting another trip to the beach."

Ellen shrugged. "Your boss keeps telling you to use up some of your vacation time, and Chelsea can make up any missing assignments when we return."

The teen smiled. At least something positive was coming out of this situation.

Cole turned to Sierra. "I know you have friends who would take you in until it's safe to go home."

"I'm not putting anyone else in danger." She stood and lifted the sleeping baby to her shoulder. "My cell phone is in my camera case. I need to call Megan to make sure she's okay. And to let her know what's going on."

"Tell you what." Cole snapped his notebook

shut. "For now, let's head back to your house. You can call your sister, then pack a bag for you and the baby."

This would give him time to call the station; Cole wanted the place dusted for prints in case Vogel had any aliases. He also wanted to check out this teddy bear. Since Vogel had squeezed it while intimidating Sierra, it wasn't a bomb, but it could be a nanny cam.

Before leaving, Sierra thanked the Andersons for their help.

"We're relieved you're okay." Hank placed his hand on her shoulder. "If you need anything while we're gone, the key is still under the ceramic turtle."

Tears returned to her eyes as she said her goodbyes.

Walking back across Sedona's rust-colored dirt in both front yards, Sierra glanced over at Cole. "I don't think Megan left the ledger copies here. They weren't with the important papers she gave me, but your officers have my permission to search my property. Anything that might put an end to this nightmare."

"With that goal in mind, I'd like to take you back to the station to go through photographs of local militia groups. I'm hoping to find a recent picture of Vogel."

She arched a brow. "Local, as in Sedona?"

"As in Arizona."

"I can do that. While I'm there, we can figure out where Danny and I should stay."

Cole followed Sierra, the baby and an officer into the house. He'd seen crime scenes in this condition of disarray but never one involving a woman he'd wanted to marry. His gaze drifted to her, and the fear in her eyes made his stomach clench. She was fortunate to be alive.

Sierra held Danny tight, staring at the chaos in her home before reaching into a camera bag for her phone. She worked around the baby to make the call to her sister and placed it on speakerphone.

"Hello there," a man answered in a mocking tone. Her expression twisted into a state of horror. "You know what happens if you give my papers to those cops, Sierra."

TWO

Thirty minutes later, Sierra crossed the police station's employee parking lot, carrying Danny in his infant seat while Cole led the way. She ignored the pain in her arm where Vogel had kicked her. It didn't feel as bad as it had an hour ago.

What troubled Sierra the most was not hearing from her sister. A murderer had Megan's cell phone. Cole had contacted the New Orleans Police Department before leaving the house, but they had no information—yet.

A glance at the baby confirmed he was warm and content, looking up at the puffy clouds in the sky, while she had goose bumps born of fear traveling down her arms despite wearing a long black sweater. Scanning the surrounding vehicles and landscape beyond the fenced property, she searched for any sign of Vogel. Was he watching her? What would he do if he knew she was here with a detective?

Cole shifted the suitcase and diaper bag he was holding and opened the back door. Inside the police station, they walked down a long hall and turned into a room divided by office partitions. The cowboy boots he wore with his gray Western suit made shuffling noises as they transitioned onto commercial-grade carpeting.

"Here we go." He placed her belongings in the corner of his cubicle and gestured for her to sit. "By any chance, do you have Megan's Yuma address?"

She shook her head, feeling foolish for not knowing basic information about her sister. It showed how far apart they'd grown since that awful night ten years ago, when they'd screamed at each other until neither could stand to be in the same room together. If only she could go back in time…

"No worries," Cole said, not allowing his opinion on the matter to show in his expression.

By the time she reached the chair across from Cole's desk, her nephew had begun to fuss. Sierra unfastened the carrier's straps and gathered him into her arms. "It's okay, sweetie. I'm here." She rocked Danny until he settled and closed his eyes. Too much excitement was probably overwhelming him. She knew what it was doing to her. "Everything will be all right," she whispered, hoping her words were true.

Cole booted up his computer. The only other object on his desk was a small plant. There were no framed photos, but four plaques hung on the partition wall—diplomas and commendations. He typed, then turned the monitor so they could both view the screen. "This is Vogel's driver's license picture."

Sierra stared into the dark, steely eyes projected from the screen and shuddered. It took her a moment to recover before noticing the man didn't have a beard then and was at least ten years younger. She pointed out the differences, then turned away, not wanting to look at his face any longer than necessary.

"This won't take long, I promise."

She bobbed her head while wrapping her sweater tighter around her body. *Why is this happening?* She'd tried so hard to live a calm, safe life.

Cole soon turned the screen toward her once again. "These are surveillance pictures taken during a militia gathering. If you recognize Vogel in any of them, let me know."

He patiently waited as she studied each picture. When she shook her head, he scrolled to the next one. She'd almost given up hope when she spotted the man who had attacked her. His glasses and goatee were unmistakable. "There!" She pointed at what reminded her of a class picture, except each of the dozen men, lined up in two rows, wore camouflage and carried an assault rifle. "That's him. The one on the right."

"You're sure?" Cole ran a hand through his thick, dark hair. His amber eyes—a rare shade she'd never seen on anyone else—met her gaze from across the desk.

"Positive. And he looks exactly the same as he did today." Sierra noticed the fierce determination evident in each man in the photograph. Had Vogel come alone to Sedona? Or were members of his militia group hiding nearby, waiting for him to call them into action?

The baby stirred in her arms, and she rubbed his back, silently vowing to keep him out of his father's reach. *Father.* That man didn't deserve the privilege.

"You're doing great, Sierra." Cole turned the monitor in his direction and added, "I'm sending a copy of this picture to my contact in the Yuma Police Department. He might be able to provide more information, like the names of Vogel's associates."

"I was thinking he might not have come alone."

He studied her before saying, "It's a possibility, but we'll be ready for them." After she nodded, he removed his cell phone from a clip at his waist and touched the screen before lifting the device to his ear. "How's it going at the Lowery house?" Pause. "Really? Let me know if you find anything else."

Sierra sat on the edge of her seat, waiting for him to wrap up his call. "Did they find the papers Megan hid?"

"Not yet, but they did discover the teddy bear is a nanny cam."

Her stomach dropped. "Vogel was planning to spy on me?"

"We may be able to turn that bear against him. If it's okay with you, I'll ask our cyber guys to redirect the video feed. I suspect Vogel will make another visit to your house while you're gone."

"Maybe he'll bring one of his friends over and confess to the murders in front of the bear."

"Wouldn't that be nice."

Sierra watched him work on the computer, finding it difficult to believe she was sitting across the desk from Cole Walker. She'd always known he would make an outstanding law enforcement officer. He had been brave, while she'd feared what the future might hold. It hadn't always been that way. Not before she lost her grandmother and then her parents. They were the people she had loved and depended on most in the world.

And now she didn't know what Vogel had

done to her sister before he took her phone. Sierra's chest tightened at the thought. She looked down into Danny's precious face. His trusting blue eyes. Her heart filled with love. Worry. Grief. Would he have to live without his mother, too?

When Cole had started at the police academy, Sierra was convinced that one day she would open the door to find an officer standing there to deliver the news that he had died in the line of duty. She couldn't live with that fear. Not then. Not now. The look of hurt on his face when she broke up with him had destroyed her, but he had apparently let go of the past and the feelings he once had for her. He was all business. If anyone could find Vogel and put him behind bars, it was this man.

Cole glanced over at her, unaware of her thoughts. "You mentioned your sister wanted to find someone in New Orleans to give her evidence to. Do you know who she had in mind?"

"Finally, a question I can answer." Her attention was drawn to Danny, who had made a tiny sound. She kissed the top of his head, breathed in that soothing baby smell, and continued, "When Megan read Vogel's ledger, she recognized the name of a woman featured in a true-crime podcast called *The Cajun Copperhead: Striking Out against Crime*. The man reporting on the story is a retired federal agent committed to exposing anyone involved in her murder. He gets his info from his contacts in law enforcement."

Cole worked his jaw. "Megan was hoping to see him?"

"More than hoping—she managed to get an appointment with him yesterday. Gator paid Vogel a lot of money for that bomb. He might be connected to people with influence. Megan was convinced the Copperhead could tell her who to trust with her evidence."

"And how did her meeting with him go?"

Dread took root in Sierra's gut. "I don't know. She told me she'd find a way to reach out to me every morning. I didn't hear from her before my photo shoot today. I wanted to call her, but she instructed me not to unless there was an emergency. And now Vogel has the prepaid cell phone she took with her. I'm scared to death."

Cole's eyes darkened, no doubt harboring the same fears. "I'll find this podcaster. I want to know if Megan showed up for her appointment."

A man with short brown wavy hair, wearing a black suit, stepped inside the office area.

"Is there something I can help you with, Detective Gold?" Cole's terse tone hung in the air.

"Can I have a moment of your time? Out in

the hall?" He nodded to Sierra as if apologizing for the interruption.

"I'm a bit busy here." Not once did Cole glance away from the keyboard and monitor, giving off the impression that Gold made a habit of interrupting. "Can it wait?"

"No, it can't." Detective Gold rubbed his chin with the pad of his thumb. "I've officially been assigned this case."

"What?" The word escaped Sierra's mouth before she could stop herself. Danny squirmed, and she rocked him back and forth. "This has to be some sort of mistake."

Gold shot Cole a look that said they should have spoken away from her, out in the hall, as he'd wanted. "It's come to the lieutenant's attention that the two of you know each other," he told Sierra. "It would be better for all concerned if you had a detective who will be seen as…" He glanced at Cole as he ended with "impartial."

His comment sparked her anger.

"Cole is both professional and impartial." Now she fully understood Megan's need to find a trusted ally. Sierra didn't know this Gold guy. Would he care more about finding the evidence than protecting her and the baby? She held Danny close while turning to Cole for help. "Do something, *please*, Cole. I don't want anyone else in charge."

* * *

Cole's gaze turned to the infant, who may be Sierra's only living relative. He had to make sure he protected them both. No matter what the other detective said. Jeff Gold, the lieutenant's cousin, had been hired a month ago. He was good at his job, but he didn't know Sierra. If she didn't have faith in Gold's instincts or decisions, her fear might make her flee to deal with matters on her own.

"Detective Gold, let's finish this conversation out in the hall." Cole stood. He should have dealt with this in private a minute ago, but he didn't want to spend a second on anything other than finding Megan and putting Sierra's attacker behind bars.

"After you." Gold gestured toward the door, his expression deadpan.

To say the man's presence bothered Cole was an understatement. Gold had replaced a detective who retired two months ago. Before that, he worked for the Phoenix Police Department. The lieutenant had made it clear his cousin was on a fast track to a supervisory position and expected everyone around him to help make that possible. As a result, the new detective was assigned the types of challenging cases that were once given to Cole.

And with Sedona's rapidly growing population, the department was about to hire a detective from Chicago with over ten years of experience. Cole had an excellent track record for solving cases, but he had never worked in a big city. These detectives might have skills he didn't possess. He worried he could end up with nothing but stolen bicycles and pickpocketing cases. But then, he did have one advantage over them: he'd grown up in Sedona and knew it like the back of his hand.

Gold lit into him after they were beyond earshot. "What were you thinking? You went out on a call to your college girlfriend's house?"

"I see the rumor mill is working overtime—as usual."

"Are you denying you two dated?"

"No, I'm not. But if you try to tell me you wouldn't have done the same thing, I'll have trouble believing you. Besides, you were already out working a burglary. I was available."

"That doesn't change the possibility that an effective prosecutor might make accusations of impropriety based on your personal interest in the case. For that reason, it's already been decided that I'll handle things from here."

Cole hated to admit the man was right. Any arrest would have to be made by Gold.

The dispatch supervisor marched up to them. "The mounted patrol found abandoned backpacks left in five different tourist locations. Sounds like a possible terrorist threat to me."

"Or teens with a warped sense of humor," Gold suggested.

The mounted unit was composed of volunteers, like Cole's brother Zach, who was working at their family's ranch today. He'd led several local search and rescue operations during his time with the unit.

"Remind the patrol officers securing each of the five areas to keep everyone far away from those backpacks." The lieutenant, a severe-looking career man, had stepped out of his office in time to hear their conversation. "I've called in the Flagstaff bomb squad."

"Yes, sir." The supervisor disappeared behind a nearby door.

Bomb squad. Trepidation twisted in Cole's gut.

"The chief wants to see you both in his office." The lieutenant's gaze shifted between the detectives. "Take Miss Lowery with you."

"Right away." Gold watched the lieutenant leave.

Cole wondered why the chief wanted to see both detectives and Sierra, especially if the case had been reassigned. "You want to take the diaper bag or the baby?"

Gold raised a brow. "I don't think your girlfriend wants me handling either."

"Not my girlfriend—and you're right. She wouldn't. Meet you there." Cole found Sierra playing with Danny. The baby giggled when she blew softly on his face.

Cole grinned. The kid was too cute. And Sierra was still as pretty as the day he'd met her after church one Sunday. Regretfully, she'd stopped attending services after her parents passed away, just when she needed the support the most.

She glanced up at him. Her wide eyes filled with hopeful anticipation. "What's the verdict?"

"The chief wants to see us, so I guess we'll find out together." He picked up the infant carrier and diaper bag.

"One second. I need to get something." She lifted Danny to her shoulder, then removed a pacifier from a side pocket in the bag. "This will make it easier to hear the discussion. He was fed and changed right before I picked him up, and now that he's had a nap, he'll demand attention."

Cole was surprised Sierra hadn't found a man with a safe, steady job to marry. She was a natural mother and had always wanted children of her own.

He didn't know why he was questioning her marital status when he hadn't taken the leap, either. With his erratic work schedule, he'd canceled more dates than he went on. And if any woman expressed concern over the dangers involved with his job, he stopped seeing her. He never wanted a repeat of what had happened with Sierra.

She smiled fondly at the baby. "I'm discovering Danny's predictable even during chaotic times."

Predictable. The quality he most admired.

He ushered her to the chief's office, where they were introduced to FBI special agents Albers and Fisher. Both wore dark suits, but Albers was much taller than his colleague. Maybe six foot two. He offered Sierra a chair near theirs, in front of the chief's mahogany desk. She glanced back at Cole before sitting, still holding the baby up to her shoulder.

"I'll be over here." He gestured toward Detective Gold, who stood off to the side.

"Thank you for joining us, Miss Lowery," the chief said, his tone kind yet professional. His full head of gray hair was a reminder of the many years he'd served on the force. "These agents are from the Flagstaff field office."

Fisher, an older man in his late forties or early fifties, chimed in, "Your sister, Megan, was supposed to meet us here to hand over evidence, proving her boyfriend, Oliver Vogel, is responsible for the deaths of five people, including a

Louisiana judge. She'd discussed the bombing with a podcaster before calling us, but you already know that."

Sierra's jaw dropped. Apparently, Megan had failed to mention that the "hot target" Vogel had discussed with Gator was a judge.

The fact that Megan had kept secrets from her sister came as no surprise to Cole.

"Are you all right?" He stepped closer, ready to spring forward if needed.

Her gaze locked on his. "I'm worried about my sister."

"As are we," Agent Albers confessed. "Your sister told our agent that she had to fly back to Arizona to collect copies of a ledger hidden in Sedona. When we tried to confirm our meeting for today, her phone went to voice mail. She never called us back. And she missed her flight," he added, his tone grim.

Sierra drew in a shaky breath, and Cole had to resist the desire to pull up a chair and sit next to her, as any caring friend would. His professionalism was already in question, at least by Detective Gold.

"Did Megan say why she left the papers here instead of taking them with her?" Sierra winced when Danny pulled strands of her hair. She removed them from his grip and then placed him on her lap.

"She did not." Agent Fisher ignored the baby and continued, "Have you heard from your sister?"

Sierra responded with only a slight shake of her head before her gaze drifted in Cole's direction. He told them about Vogel answering the phone when she tried to reach out to Megan— information he'd already shared with the chief.

The agents exchanged troubled looks, and then Agent Fisher spoke. "We've suspected that Oliver Vogel was a contract killer, specializing in car bombs. Last year, he was in Dallas when a car bomb was sent down a hill into the house of a reporter. It blew up on impact. Unfortunately, we've never had enough evidence to convict him. This is our chance."

Realization hit Cole head-on.

"Chief." He stepped up to the desk, hurrying to explain. "The backpacks. They're a diversion. I'm sure of it."

"What do you mean?"

"The five backpacks left in tourist areas are meant to divert our resources. Vogel wants every available officer deployed elsewhere." Cole maintained an even tone for Sierra's sake.

The chief grabbed his phone. "Lieutenant, I want someone monitoring the security feed from outside the station."

Sierra's eyes widened as she put the pieces

together. "He's coming after us! We need to leave. Now."

When she tried to flee, Cole couldn't hang back any longer. He raced to beat her to the door and placed his hands gently on her shoulders. His gaze locked on hers. "No matter what Vogel has planned, you're both safe here. There are five law enforcement officers surrounding you."

Sierra surveyed the room and eased back into the chair. "I guess you're right," she said, but her expression belied her words.

"I understand your concern," Agent Fisher said in a softer tone. "And I agree it would be better if we took you away from the station. And we will. Soon. First, we need to make sure Vogel isn't waiting for us. Then there's something we need your help with."

Cole guessed what came next.

Agent Fisher kept his focus on Sierra. "Once we put Vogel and his accomplice, Gator, behind bars, you'll no longer have to look over your shoulder. What we need is for the three of us to go back to your house to search for those copies of the ledger and passports."

"Don't forget the fake driver's licenses. The police already looked," Sierra stated emphatically. "And I don't want to go back to the house until you have Vogel in custody. If you want to know where those papers are, find my sister and ask her."

"We have agents looking for your sister, ma'am," Agent Albers explained. "In the meantime, we do need your help to put this man away, or he'll kill again. You are more familiar with Megan's interests and daily activities than anyone else. You can figure out where she hid the evidence."

They obviously didn't know that, up until recently, the sisters hadn't spoken to each other in ten years.

"I'll arrange a police escort," the chief added matter-of-factly.

Cole touched the baby's shoulder, reminding them what was at stake. "What kind of protection are you offering Miss Lowery?"

Agent Fisher arched a brow, as if wondering about Cole's relationship with Sierra. "We'll stay with Miss Lowery during the search for evidence. Once Vogel is behind bars, she can return to her normal life."

"But he's in a militia group," Sierra protested.

"That's true," Agent Fisher said, his tone even-keeled. "But they won't have any reason to go after you. You're not a witness to their activities or Vogel's murders. It's the copies of the ledger that will put him away for life, not your testimony."

Sierra nodded her understanding. "I don't think I'll be of much help, but I'll go with you if Detective Walker can come with us."

Agent Fisher furrowed his brow.

Cole turned toward the chief, who shook his head no. His stomach sank. Sierra was scared and needed his help. He was about to ask for vacation time when the desk phone rang.

The chief answered. "You're sure?" Pause. "Okay, let me know if you see anything." He hung up and addressed the agents. "Vogel's not out there."

Detective Gold stepped forward. "I'll stand guard outside, just in case."

A chirp escaped Sierra's purse, and she reached inside for her phone. "The text is from my sister's burner phone. The one Vogel has." Sierra drew in a steadying breath before swiping the screen and reading, "Don't go with those agents—or else." Terror filled her eyes, and she tossed the device across the chief's desk. It hit the back wall with a thud. "He can hear us!"

The baby whimpered, then cried.

"Vogel heard or read the messages the agents left for your sister. He knew they would be here." The chief snatched up her phone. A crack ran diagonally across the screen. "Don't worry, young lady. He's just trying to scare you."

"And he's doing a great job." The baby's cries

turned to wails. She hugged him against her chest and patted his back. "I'm sorry, sweetie. This is all too much for you. For the both of us."

Agent Fisher turned away from the noise and stretched his hand out across the desk. "We might be able to use this phone to track Vogel."

After the chief handed it over, Agent Albers stood. "Even if Vogel's not here at the station, we'll take extra precautions by sneaking Miss Lowery out the back way to a side road. Fewer witnesses." He addressed his colleague, "I'll pull the car up to the door, and you can help her with the baby. Detective Gold, come with me."

Sierra turned to Cole. "I don't like this."

"I know." He wanted to make it all go away for her and Danny, but he couldn't. He turned back to the chief. "Can I—"

"No." He dismissed Cole by directing his attention elsewhere.

The agents and Gold headed for the hall.

Danny continued to express his discontent—loudly. Sierra lifted him up, off her shoulder. "Where's your pacifier? No wonder you're upset." She searched the carpeted floor.

"It might have fallen on our way over here," Cole said. "I'll go check."

"I'll go with you." Tears rolled down the baby's cheeks as she rewrapped the blanket around him. On the way out, she told the agents where they were going and that they'd be right back.

Holding the baby close, Sierra walked with Cole, who carried her belongings down the long hall to his office, where they found the pacifier near a chair. He placed the carrier on top of his desk and reached for the little plastic handle. The ground suddenly jerked, and a nerve-racking boom thundered from outside the building.

Sierra lost her balance, shrieked and fell, keeping the baby pressed against her chest. Cole instinctively lunged forward, preventing them from slamming against the wall. He bumped his shoulder as he fell beside her but didn't give it a second thought. He'd felt much worse many times before.

"Are you okay?" They huddled together, anticipating another explosion, while he checked her and Danny over for apparent injuries.

"I think so." Sierra kissed the baby's cheek, but he kept whimpering, frightened by their tumble.

Once Cole was fairly certain a second bomb wouldn't go off, he pushed to his feet and headed toward the door. He needed to assess the damage and their new level of danger. "Stay here."

"Don't leave us," her plea followed him out into the hall.

A single glance confirmed what he had feared.

At the far end, beyond the back door—now hanging from a single hinge—were the remains of a smoldering car. His chest tightened.

He wanted to check for survivors, but his training warned him not to leave Sierra unguarded.

THREE

The blast had knocked Sierra off her feet. Afraid to move, she remained seated on the carpeted floor of Cole's office, holding the baby protectively against her chest. Her pulse had skyrocketed. Danny cried uncontrollably, his legs kicking out beneath him. The roar of the explosion, combined with their fall, had scared them both, but thankfully they were physically uninjured. No scrapes or sprains. Their emotional well-being was a different matter.

Cole stood outside his office's partitioned wall, speaking on his cell phone and keeping guard over them.

"Everything will be okay," Sierra promised Danny, but she knew if she didn't find those papers and hand them over, she would become Vogel's next target. "Shh." With her back pressed against the wall, her hands shook as she tucked the yellow blanket around her nephew.

Vogel was a bomber. Whatever just happened had to be his handiwork. That's why he'd warned her not to leave with the FBI agents. He didn't kill her—this time. There was no guarantee he wouldn't take her life once he had what he wanted. She was in a no-win situation. Panic hit her like lightning strikes. She forced her mind to focus on the baby as her body trembled.

"We'll be okay," she repeated, trying to convince them both. Sirens, coming and going, drowned out the sound of their sobs. She buried her head into the baby's neck, hoping no one had died in the explosion but fearing they had.

Soon, Danny's cries softened to a whimper. Sierra scooted closer to the diaper bag and removed a pacifier wipe from a side zipper compartment. After a quick cleaning, she offered him this additional source of comfort. Worn out from crying, he sucked while fighting to keep his eyes open.

Her nephew's blond curls reminded Sierra of his mother. "Megan…" She struggled to maintain a glimmer of hope. "Please be hiding from Vogel. Danny needs you."

The alternative was more than Sierra could bear.

Cole strode over and crouched beside them, his grim expression a prelude to his statement. "The agents' car was rigged with a bomb."

Grief washed over her. "Were they…"

"Critically injured. Detective Gold, too. They were walking across the parking lot when Agent Fisher started the car with a fob. It exploded immediately. Their wounds are severe, but they're alive. The EMTs are prepping them for transport."

Would any of this have been avoided if she hadn't come to the police station? "Oh, Cole, this is all my fault."

He gently cupped her jaw, drawing her attention to his handsome face. "Don't think that for even a second. This is all on Vogel. He's a vicious man."

Sierra looked into Cole's amber eyes, thankful he was there to protect them.

"Are you ready to move to a chair? You might be more comfortable."

Weighed down by grief, she couldn't budge other than to care for the baby. "Not yet."

The chief of police entered the office, his tone severe as he wrapped up a conversation on his radio. "Walker, I need you to get Miss Lowery and her nephew out of Sedona. The FBI will send more agents, but in the meantime, it's our responsibility to keep them out of this bomber's reach."

Cole hesitated as if considering the fact that

he'd just been taken off the case because he wasn't seen as an impartial investigator.

"You're the only one here with this kind of experience," the chief explained. "You kept a witness alive when drug traffickers wanted to kill her. That was no easy feat."

"Yes, sir. You can count on me."

Sierra was relieved Cole would stay with her, but leaving Sedona scared her to death. Despite the bombing, she felt safer in the police station surrounded by law enforcement officers than out there, where Vogel lurked. Watching. Waiting.

A quick check of the clock on the wall had her heart racing even faster. "I have forty-three hours left to hand over the papers. If he wanted me dead now, he wouldn't have warned me not to leave with the agents. Can't we wait here?"

The chief rubbed his forehead and then spoke to her in the same soft, calm tone her father had used when telling her why she couldn't have her way. "I've been dealing with men like this Vogel character for over thirty years. They change their minds without rhyme or reason. It's better if he doesn't know where you're hiding. We don't want to take any chances with your life—or the baby's."

Sirens announced the departure of another emergency vehicle. Danny's eyes and mouth opened for a second before he sucked the pacifier and lowered his lids again. The warm bundle in Sierra's arms had to be fiercely protected.

"Any suggestions?" Cole asked the chief, reminding her of the matter at hand—escaping to a safer location.

"Walker, your father called," the chief said, easing into his answer. "Sedona is a small town at heart, and we've gotten to know each other over the years. He heard what happened at Miss Lowery's house and offered the use of your family ranch. I can't think of a safer place. If you're okay with Miss Lowery and the baby staying there, I'll ask the sheriff for help. I know he'll send deputies. We can turn the ranch into a fortress."

"Does my father know about the bomb?"

The chief nodded. "He does. We spoke only minutes ago."

Cole furrowed his brow, most likely wondering why his father hadn't called him directly. "I want to make sure my family fully understands the situation."

Sierra had heard about that drug ring burning down the barn at Cole's family ranch and didn't want anything else happening to them because of her. "This isn't a good idea. Someone might get hurt."

"No matter where we go, someone might get

hurt," Cole said, "especially if we stay in Sedona. At least the ranch is out of town. Plus, every member of my family can shoot a gun and hit their targets. And it's only until the FBI gets here. We're talking hours, not days."

His argument made sense, but she wished no one needed to put their lives on the line for them.

Cole headed away from the partition walls of his office, phone in hand.

The chief stepped closer. "You're doing a fine job." He smiled at Danny. "Hang in there, Miss Lowery. The FBI will capture this guy. You'll see."

Sierra wasn't looking forward to the time when the FBI would once again take over the investigation. Cole wouldn't be able to stay with her then. She knew his character and trusted him. From what she'd seen so far, he hadn't changed much over the past twelve years. He was still the honest, dependable man she had once dated. His whole family was that way. They were good people. If Cole had chosen a safer career, she would be married to him by now.

Cole disconnected his call and addressed the chief. "My family not only agreed to have Sierra and Danny at the ranch, they insisted."

The chief clapped his hands together. "Great!

I'll call the sheriff right away. We want those deputies in place as soon as possible. In the meantime, we need a plan to sneak the three of you out of here without the bomber knowing."

Cole lifted his finger. "Taken care of. My brother Zach will meet us at the new emergency center. I was thinking we could pretend Sierra needs medical assistance, and then, while everyone thinks she's being treated, we can sneak her out a back door to a waiting SUV."

The chief worked his jaw, apparently mulling over the plan. "Let me arrange the transportation to the center, and I'll tell the press a young woman was injured in the explosion. If we're buying time to hide her, let's let Vogel think she needs more than a bandage. I'll send backup along, just in case. That'll keep Vogel from going inside the center." The chief turned to Sierra. "We'll have you two in more comfortable surroundings in no time."

"What about the forty-three hours I have left to hand over the papers?" Sierra asked, concerned about what the bomber would do if she failed to deliver.

"He can't hurt you if he can't find you," the chief surmised. "And once the FBI agents in New Orleans find Megan, they'll hide her in a safe house until these guys are behind bars."

"One more thing." Cole held up a set of keys.

"I need the base for this baby carrier in the back seat of my car."

"On it." The chief caught the keys. Before leaving, he paused long enough to state, "All communication goes through me from this moment forward."

"Understood." Cole's tone reflected the severity of their situation.

The disturbing sounds of people rushing about and loud, rushed conversations streamed in through the open door before it shut. "Cole, how bad was the explosion?" She cringed at her awkward question. The bomb had obviously been bad. They had said the agents and Detective Gold were critically injured. "What I'm asking is, if anyone else was hurt?"

He shook his head. "That's one good thing about Vogel's backpack distraction. Every available officer is in town, keeping people far away from what might be more bombs."

"When will you know what's in the backpacks?"

"The Flagstaff bomb squad will be here soon."

Before her parents' deaths, she would have prayed there were no more explosives. By the time she'd buried them, she was convinced God had abandoned her family and left praying to other people. Those who still believed He cared.

Minutes later, a redheaded man wearing a blue EMT uniform stepped into the office. "Miss Lowery, I'm Fred Miller. The chief asked me to escort you out of here in my ambulance."

Cole flashed his badge. "The baby and I will be riding along with her."

"Understood." The tall, lanky man's gaze zeroed in on her neck. "How are you feeling? Anything hurt?"

"We weren't near the explosion," she explained, resisting the urge to cover the marks Vogel had left when he'd squeezed her throat.

"But you were attacked at the house." Cole reached down for Danny. "It wouldn't hurt to let him look you over before we leave."

"I'm fine." She handed Cole the baby but only to make it easier to push up off the floor. "How is this going to work?"

EMT Fred gestured over his shoulder. "I have a gurney in the hall. With your permission, I'll strap you in and roll you out to the ambulance."

"I'll bring the baby with us," Cole assured her. "He'll always be close to you."

"Don't leave me." She wasn't asking.

"I won't," he promised, holding Danny with natural ease. The Walkers had a large extended family. It was common for cousins to visit the ranch with their children, including infants.

A thought occurred to her. "Did Detective

Gold and the agents already leave? I don't want to take transportation someone else needs."

The baby stared up at Cole as he spoke. "They're already on their way to the hospital. From there, they'll most likely be flown to Phoenix. Now, the sooner our EMT here gets us to the medical center, which isn't far, the sooner he'll be free to help someone else in the community."

"Then let's go." A new sense of urgency propelled her forward. She touched Danny's fingers before heading out the office door. The EMT helped her into a sitting position on the gurney. He then strapped her in and covered the lower half of her body with a blanket, presumably so no one could see she hadn't been injured.

Cole exited the office door, carrying their bags and Danny, secured in his carrier. The chubby-cheeked baby who had been inconsolable earlier was now babbling while surveying his surroundings. "We'll need to head out the front door."

She almost asked why but then realized the back door led to the parking lot where the bomb had gone off. With her head leaning back against the gurney, she studied the ceiling, willing away the terrible images invading her mind.

Another man wearing dark blue slacks and a matching-colored T-shirt introduced himself as Officer Thomas. "I'll be your driver." He glanced over at Cole. "The chief thought it would be a good idea to have someone out of uniform behind the wheel."

"Trust the chief to think of everything." Cole touched Sierra's arm. "Are you ready?"

"As much as I can be under the circumstances." She nervously glanced about, searching for Vogel as Fred and Officer Thomas pushed her gurney toward the front of the police station.

She'd rather walk out on her own two feet, but everyone seemed to think this was for the best. And they were probably right. If Vogel didn't know where to find them because he thought she was receiving treatment, then he might not try some underhanded attempt to force her to find the papers sooner. He was desperate for them. They provided enough proof to tie him to each bombing death and allow law enforcement to seize his bank accounts.

When the front doors opened, the bright light stung her eyes. Sierra turned her head to block out the sun as the EMT connected the gurney to a contraption that lifted her into the back of the ambulance. She was amazed at how effortless it all seemed.

Once the gurney was in place, Cole climbed in, carrying the baby. The chief handed over his keys and the base to Danny's car seat, which was used to secure him into a back-facing position behind her.

Cole shifted over to the cushioned bench at her side. The EMT placed their bags inside and closed the doors.

The ambulance jostled a bit before the engine turned over. Nerve-wracking anxiety had Sierra clenching her teeth. She leaned to the side to look back at Danny, who was busy touching his toes.

"We'll be there soon," Cole said. "The center is only a few miles away."

"And this is all necessary? I would rather not be strapped into this gurney."

"It's not that bad. Consider it your seat belt. You can't be moving around the ambulance while we're on the road in case another driver hits us."

"Like Vogel," she surmised. A shiver pulsated across her shoulders.

Cole squeezed her hand. "Like I said, the center is close. By the time I got you out of the gurney, it would be time to get you back in."

"Tricking Vogel so we can sneak over to the ranch seems too much to hope for," Sierra said with a sigh. "I just want this to be over."

"And it will be, soon." Cole sat back, stretched

the seat belt across his body and snapped it into place.

A few minutes later, Officer Thomas called back to Cole from his driver's seat. "This bomber has glasses and a gray goatee, right?"

"Yes." The hair on Cole's neck stood on end. "Why?"

"He's following us."

Sierra gripped the sides of the gurney as her heart thundered in her chest.

Cole's senses heightened. Every muscle tensed. After unhooking his seat belt, he briefly touched Sierra's hand on his way to the ambulance's back window—a simple reminder that he was there for her and would deal with this situation. He spared a glance at the baby, lulled to sleep by the motion of the moving ambulance. At least he wouldn't feel the fear hanging in the air.

Peering around the large medical decals on the window, Cole first spotted the officer following them. Beyond the police cruiser was a couple driving a sedan. Two young girls played catch with a stuffed toy animal in the back seat.

And behind the carefree family—the bomber. Vogel looked just like his militia photo.

Cole's pulse hitched. His eyes narrowed, bringing Vogel into focus like a target. If only he could capture the monster that very second.

"Thomas," Cole called out to the officer driving the ambulance. "We need to lose this guy without making it obvious. I don't want him suspecting a ruse." The traffic in the parallel lane was heavy enough to keep Vogel blocked in. They just needed a plan.

"So no sirens?" the EMT in the passenger seat asked.

"Only as a last resort. We don't want him to think she took a turn for the worse." Their intention was for Vogel to think Sierra's injuries weren't life-threatening. If he thought she wasn't physically capable of finding the papers within his timeline, he might take drastic measures to kidnap her so he could torture her into telling him where the evidence might be hidden.

A glance confirmed the baby still slept peacefully in his carrier secured to the chair behind the gurney—directly across from the back window. With Sierra and Danny on board, Cole had to avoid a shoot-out at all costs.

"We have a green light up ahead, but judging by the countdown on the crosswalk sign, it's about to change," Officer Thomas tossed back over his shoulder.

"Let's try to hit it at the end of yellow."

"Got it." The ambulance slowed.

Cole called his friend, who was driving the police cruiser. "David, the bomber is a car length behind you in the white van. We're about to try to lose him."

"The light turned yellow," Thomas interrupted. They had seconds to time this perfectly.

"David, keep the bomber from getting through the light."

"On our mark," Thomas announced. "Get set."

Sierra gripped the gurney railings. Her angst-filled expression mirrored the feelings Cole suppressed to do his job.

"Go." At the last second, Thomas picked up speed and continued through the intersection.

The officer in the cruiser braked at the crosswalk. The family rolled to a stop behind him. Vogel swerved into the now-empty parallel lane as the light turned red. Undeterred, he sped forward.

Suddenly, a black SUV shot across the intersection from the other direction, forcing the bomber to make a sharp right turn around the corner and into a mini-mart parking lot on his passenger side. Cole pressed his face closer to the window to get a better look at the driver of the SUV and grinned. "Jackson."

"Your brother Jackson?" Sierra asked incredulously.

"That's the one." Cole turned to the officer driving the ambulance. "Turn left as soon as you reach a side street that can get us to the medical center."

Sierra shook her head in disbelief. "How did Jackson know we needed help?"

"I'm not sure, but we'll find out soon." Cole peered out through the back window again. Vogel's car wasn't in the parking lot any longer. He must have reentered the street, but a busy stream of cross-traffic kept him out of the intersection. "We have about a three-minute lead on him. We'll have to move fast when we reach the medical center."

"Then unstrap me now," Sierra insisted.

"We have to carry you out of the ambulance on the gurney to make it look real. If I need you to run, I'll unfasten the straps. I promise."

Sierra blew an exasperated breath. "Okay. I understand."

Cole's phone pinged with a text. "It's from my other brother, Zach. He's waiting for us by the front doors."

Her silent nod of acknowledgment made him wonder if she was reluctant to see his family again, especially when they had all expected her to become a Walker. Cole's gaze drifted to the sleeping baby, whose vulnerability reminded him of why he'd joined the police force. *God, please give me the strength and guidance needed to keep Sierra and Danny safe.*

After two left turns, Cole peered out the window again and recognized the neighborhood. "We're almost there." He turned to Sierra, his mind wanting to reject this new reality where the kind woman he had once dated for three years was now running from a murderer. "Thomas and the EMT will handle the gurney and take you inside. I'll carry in the baby. Remember, you're playing injured."

She nodded. "Do you want silence or groaning?"

He couldn't help but smile. "Let's stick with silence for now."

"You afraid I might overact?"

He tilted his head and smiled. "Something like that."

The ambulance drove past the twenty-four-hour pharmacy and home medical–supply store, then came to a stop in front of the emergency center's double doors. Officer Thomas jumped out, opened the back end and removed their bags. While the EMT pushed the button to lower the gurney, Cole unhooked the infant carrier and the base that turned it into a car seat. After handing those pieces to Officer Thomas, he brought Danny out of the ambulance.

The building's automatic doors opened, providing an unobstructed view of Zach. His boots clacked on the concrete as he approached. He gave Sierra a nod before saying, "Nice to see you again." He paused. "Sort of. You know what I mean. Bomber and all." Zach reached for their bags and then the car seat base. "I'll take that."

"Nice to see you, too," Sierra said with a cringe. "Sorry about the bomber and all."

Officer Thomas and the EMT pushed the gurney inside. Cole followed and caught sight of Jackson rushing toward them from the other end of the long corridor. Both of his brothers wore brown Stetsons over their dark hair, long-sleeved shirts tucked into jeans and cowboy boots. Zach was the oldest, the tallest and the biggest flirt.

The twentysomething woman behind the registration desk lifted a brow and smiled as she glanced from one cowboy to the other. Cole turned to their driver, Officer Thomas. "Please remind her of HIPAA laws. No one is to be told anything at all. Then keep an eye out for Vogel at this entrance."

While the officer walked over to the desk, a middle-aged nurse joined them. "The chief called. I'm your escort."

"Thank you for your help," Cole said. "We're in a hurry."

"Let's go." The nurse and EMT pushed the gurney down the hall at a clipped pace.

Sierra kept her lips pressed together, her gaze

flitting from one person to another and then behind toward the parking lot, where Vogel could appear at any moment.

Jackson turned to Zach. "Run ahead to get the car ready, and I'll keep an eye out for trouble." After years with the DEA and now as supervisor over a Northern Arizona task force, the youngest brother was used to doling out orders in times of crisis.

Zach took it in stride and hurried ahead of them. Since Cole didn't know where they were parked or what they had discussed earlier, he wasn't in a place to offer alternative suggestions. He followed their lead, grateful for the assistance.

While rushing down the corridor and maintaining a tight grip on the infant carrier, Cole asked Jackson, "How did you know to block the intersection?"

"Zach called to tell me what was going down, and I happened to be working in town today. I looked up the guy's police record to get a visual." Jackson swerved around a cart in the hall as he spoke. "His father was a demolitions expert in the army until his dishonorable discharge for punching a superior officer. He bought land outside Yuma and taught his son everything he knew before passing away a few years ago."

"And you just happened to be at that intersection?"

"I was on my way here to help when I spotted the ambulance and your guy following you. When he tried to catch up, I cut him off," Jackson said with a chuckle. "Once he was out of the way, I hightailed it over here."

Sierra glanced up at him. "Thank you. You could have been hurt."

Jackson sent her a warm smile. "Now, don't you go worrying about us. We were born to deal with guys like this."

Her worried gaze, landing on Cole, was another reminder of the past. His job was all about stopping the Vogels of the world. That fact had scared her—still did, by the look in her eyes. Even if she depended on him for now.

When they reached the door at the opposite end of the building, the EMT removed Sierra's restraints.

"Wait here while I look outside," Jackson instructed.

As the door closed behind him, the nurse and EMT helped Sierra off the gurney.

Cole stepped between Sierra and the door, still holding the sleeping baby. "Thank you both for your help."

"I hope you get to your destination safely,"

the nurse said, assisting with the gurney. "I'll keep the talk and rumors here to a minimum."

"Be careful behind the wheel," the EMT added. "I don't want to drive you back here today."

"I hear you." Cole waved as they retreated down the hall. A knock on the door signaled the all clear. His gaze locked on Sierra's. "Stay close."

He scanned the partially filled parking lot as they hurried toward the black SUV waiting at the curb.

Jackson grabbed the infant carrier and secured the baby in the back seat. Cole rushed Sierra to the other side and opened the door for her. Once she was inside, seated next to Danny, he jumped up into the front passenger seat.

"I'll follow you," Jackson said through Zach's open window before jogging away.

They were driving away from the building, down one of the parking lot aisles in front of the pharmacy, when Cole spotted a white van turning into the medical center's main entrance. His pulse skipped a beat. "We have trouble."

FOUR

Sierra jerked around in her seat to stare out the SUV's dark-tinted window. Her heart pounded so fast she could hear the thundering rhythm in her ears. "Is that Vogel? In the white van?"

"It's him." From the front passenger seat, Cole removed his black cowboy hat and placed it on the center console. His brother Zach followed suit, then gripped the steering wheel with both hands as if ready to race through the streets of Sedona.

Sierra didn't need to be a detective to know why they removed their hats. Vogel probably witnessed her leaving the police station with a cowboy. Most of Sedona's residents and visitors wore casual clothing, nothing Western. "What about Jackson? Should you tell him to take off his Stetson? Vogel might have caught a glimpse of who ran him off the road back at the intersection."

"Jackson already did." Cole pointed to the exit at the far end of the parking lot. "Zach, over there, and don't speed."

While Cole called the chief, Sierra's gaze shifted to a mother and daughter exiting the pharmacy's automatic doors. The smiling little girl was no older than five years of age. If Vogel recognized Jackson, suspected he had been tricked and gave chase, innocent bystanders might become collateral damage. "Should Jackson go out a different exit?"

This time, Zach answered, "If the bomber heads our way, Jackson will distract him. Don't worry. He knows what he's doing."

She'd heard Jackson was a law enforcement officer, so she took Zach at his word.

Her attention returned to the SUV's back window. Vogel parked where he had a clear view of the medical center's entrance. Her gut churned. Although their ambulance driver, who was now watching the center's front door, was a highly trained police officer, she feared what might happen to him. Everywhere she looked, she spotted another potential victim.

When Cole finished his call, she asked, "Will the chief warn Officer Thomas?"

"Thomas knows what Vogel was driving, and he's expecting him." Cole's attempt to assure her failed, which he must have read on her face. "Yes, the chief will make sure he's notified."

That news should have provided a sense of comfort, but it didn't. Vogel was a contract killer. She spotted him stepping out of the van. His casual behavior disguised the evil he harbored inside. Her pulse lurched. Her breathing grew shallow. "He's going inside. Do something," she pleaded.

"I am." Cole's voice hitched. "I'm getting you out of here." The SUV bounced over the curb when they turned onto the side street and drove away from the emergency medical center. "Trust us. We have it covered."

Sirens pierced the hum of local traffic. And not just one cruiser—at least two. Maybe three.

Danny jerked. His eyelids flew open, and he protested the rude awakening with whimpers quickly shifting into loud sobs. "Now, now. Everything's okay." *Sort of.* Sierra held out his pacifier, but he pushed it away. "You must be getting hungry."

"We'll be at the ranch soon." Cole continued to watch out the back window. "Zach, make a few turns and put distance between the center and us. I'm guessing he'll hightail it out of there. Maybe even take the same exit to avoid the cruisers coming for him."

The same exit? No. She shook her head in

disbelief. How could it be this easy for Vogel to find them after they'd planned every step of this ruse to keep her ranch hideout a secret?

She peered out the window again, no longer able see the medical center or the establishments sharing the same parking lot. Between the reverberating sirens filling the SUV, Danny's cries breaking her heart and the fear ripping away her resolve, she felt like crumbling beneath an emotional weight she could no longer bear.

But she wouldn't.

Sierra looked lovingly at her nephew, tears welling at the corners of her eyes. He needed her. She could never forget that. Not even for a second.

She tried the pacifier again. He turned his face away and continued screaming. The temptation to give him a bottle in the car intensified but, according to the online parenting articles she'd read since Danny arrived, it was a choking hazard. She'd have to wait until they parked. "Hang in there, little guy."

Frustrated, she glanced out the window in time to see a white van driving through an intersection. "He's there! To our left." She pointed but not in time. "Vogel is three blocks over, traveling in the same direction down a parallel street."

"Zach, head back to the medical center."

"What?" The question escaped her lips at the same time Zach steered into a sharp U-turn. Jackson, following close behind, did the same.

"I have a plan." Cole called the chief to request an escort and notify him of Vogel's last known location.

The U-turn had surprised Danny enough that he quieted and began looking around. This time, he eagerly accepted the pacifier. The tears shining on his lashes unleashed overwhelming protective instincts she'd never felt before. They needed to reach a safe haven for her nephew's sake—before it was too late. Under no circumstances could Vogel be allowed to find them.

They entered the medical center's parking lot and drove up to a police cruiser. From the distant sounds, she surmised the other officers were pursuing Vogel. Cole rolled down the window and spoke to the driver. Sierra was surprised to see Officer Thomas sitting in the passenger seat. She only caught parts of their conversation.

"Let's head home," Cole told his brother before turning in his seat to glance back at her and Danny. "They'll hang back enough not to make it obvious you two are in this vehicle."

She tried to smile but failed. Cole went back to scouting their surroundings, and she leaned back against the seat, her heart still racing but feeling more confident. Slightly more confident. Nothing would calm her nerves completely until Vogel was behind bars. And even then, it might take months or years to feel normal again.

After what seemed like an eternity later, they reached the ranch. Finally. Two sheriff's vehicles guarded the gate, allowing only family and law enforcement to enter.

Suddenly, apprehension replaced her fear. This would be the first time she'd have to face Cole's parents since their breakup. Even if they didn't bring up the subject, it would hang in the air between them.

Cole lifted his phone to his ear. "Lily, I need a parking spot in the garage." He listened, then answered, "Thirty seconds."

Sierra had almost forgotten about the younger sister who adored her brothers. That meeting might not go well, either. She kissed the baby's head, reminding herself that enduring a few uncomfortable situations was a small price to pay for Danny's safety and comfort.

They rounded the ranch house, and the garage door lifted. Lily drove a sedan out, and Zach pulled inside next to a truck. The rattle of gears churning echoed in the enclosed space. The door descended, blocking the outside light except for where it leaked in between metal and wall.

Sierra exhaled. *Time to face the music.*

Cole opened her door and waited for her to exit before reaching for her bags. On the driver's side, Zach dealt with Danny and his carrier.

Mr. Walker opened the kitchen door for them. Other than a few more gray hairs and laugh lines, he hadn't changed much. His demeanor still reminded her of her father.

He placed a large, gentle hand on her shoulder. "Sierra, welcome back to our home."

Relief brought on by his greeting, gratitude for a secure place to stay and a deep-felt yearning for her parents washed over her in a single powerful wave. A tear slid down her cheek. "I'm so sorry. I didn't mean for any of this to happen."

He wrapped his arm around her shoulder and escorted her to the living room. "The chief told me about the bomber. None of this is your fault."

"Of course not." Cole's sister, Lily, gestured for her to sit on the sofa, where Zach placed Danny, still secured in his carrier.

Cole left the diaper bag beside the sofa and then disappeared with her travel bag down the hall.

"You are all so kind." Sierra took in their gentle expressions as she freed the baby and lifted him into her arms. "We'll only be here for a few hours."

"You're welcome to stay as long as you like." Mr. Walker motioned for Cole to follow him when he emerged from the hall, and the three men retreated into the kitchen. No doubt to talk about Vogel.

"Really, how are you doing?" Lily asked. The pencil-thin teenager with braces and ponytails had grown into an attractive woman.

"Worried. Scared. Terrified something will happen to Megan's baby." Sierra glanced down at Danny, who was shoving fingers into his mouth.

"That's understandable." Lily sat on the sofa and played peekaboo with Danny. He giggled at her antics.

"Do you want to hold him while I fix his bottle?"

"You don't have to ask me twice." Lily held him up so his feet rested on her thighs, as if he were standing on his own, which he couldn't do yet. "You'll be walking before too long." When Danny greeted her with a gurgle, she laughed. "You look just like your mommy."

Thinking of Megan had Sierra worrying again. Not wanting to lose what little resilience she had left, she focused on prepping the baby formula.

Danny eyed his bottle and waved his arms in anticipation. Sierra gathered him into her arms, glad she could now feed him. He patted the bottle as if telling her he approved.

"I heard we have a baby in the house." Mrs. Walker entered the living room from the hallway.

Cole's mother's face lit up when she spotted Danny, and Sierra's breath caught in her throat as she waited for the type of reception she would receive. Mrs. Walker had helped console Sierra after her parents were killed in the car accident. At the time, everyone had expected Sierra and Cole to get married. They had dated for three years and had made it clear that was their intention. Mrs. Walker loved her family dearly, and Sierra felt like she'd betrayed the woman who had done so much for her when she hurt her son by walking away.

Mrs. Walker's tight smile landed on Sierra. "Can I get you anything?"

Sierra's heart sank. It was silly of her to think Cole's mother might welcome her the way her husband had. "I'm fine. Thank you for your generosity. We'll be leaving as soon as the FBI gets here. I don't want to put you out."

Embarrassment flickered across the woman's face. "Please don't think we don't want you here. We do. I… I was just surprised by the feelings that flooded back when I saw you sitting here in our living room. I miss you. We all do."

"I miss you all, too. I didn't mean to hurt anyone when I left…" Sierra's gaze dropped to the baby.

"Consider it ancient history." Mrs. Walker's compassionate tone mirrored her words. "We are sincerely glad you're both here with us, and we want to help." Her gaze lingered on Danny. "He's precious."

"Mom," Lily interjected. "We should work on dinner and let them rest."

"You're right." Mrs. Walker stood. "Sierra, I have the guest room set up for you and the baby."

Relax. Easier said than done. After the women left the room, Sierra surveyed her surroundings as she continued to feed her nephew. So much of it had changed since her last visit. There used to be a beige settee where the wingback chair now stood. Memories of Cole holding her hand while watching television side by side broke through the protective barriers she'd built to forget them. Her chest tightened, and she closed her eyes.

Focus on the baby.

Danny made a sucking noise. Sierra checked to make sure he was getting enough formula. He was. She watched every move he made, awed by how he could bring so much joy to those who loved him.

Her nerves started to settle. Not as much as she'd like, but that was expected, under the circumstances. After burping Danny, Sierra propped him up with pillows in the corner of the sofa and tickled his toes. He giggled again and grabbed his feet. Her heart warmed at the sight.

Cole stepped into the living room, his expression grim as he walked over and sat down beside her.

Dread took root in her soul. Fearing the worst, Sierra pulled the baby into her arms. "What happened?"

"I'm sorry," he said. "They found Megan."

Cole watched the color drain from Sierra's face and quickly reached out to touch her arm, ready to take the baby if necessary.

Her breathing grew shallow, and fear darkened her blue eyes. "Megan's dead, isn't she?"

"I'm afraid so." He hated this part of his job. Knowing how this would affect Sierra made it much worse. "The owner of a short-term rental property found her. There were signs of a struggle."

"A rental property?" Sierra's features twisted into a mask of confusion. "She was staying at a hotel."

Cole's chest tightened, not wanting to explain, but he believed Sierra deserved the truth. "Megan's hands were bound together with zip ties."

Her eyes, wet with tears, narrowed into slits. "Vogel did this."

"Him or maybe an accomplice."

"One of his militia buddies?"

"Could be," Cole agreed. "And Vogel evaded capture near the medical center, so he's still out there."

The baby fussed, and she turned to place him back down on the pillows, as if not trusting herself to maintain her grip on him. Unaware of how much his world had just changed, Danny leaned forward to pat the sofa cushion while Sierra watched over him.

"Danny will have a hole in his heart where Megan's love had been." Her voice cracked on her words, then turned to a hoarse whisper. "I've felt that gaping hole since the day my parents died."

Cole searched for the right words but could only come up with, "I would say I understand, but we both know that's impossible. But I have lost loved ones. Turning to God always helped me through the most difficult times."

Sierra shook her head, then swiped at her tears. "I don't want to hear about God. He has taken away everyone I love. Except for Danny."

Feeling useless, Cole silently prayed for Sierra and the baby, then retrieved tissues from across the room. He left the box on the coffee table within her reach, then returned to the sofa, hoping his mere presence would help her realize she wasn't alone.

When the baby began to whimper, she placed the pacifier in his mouth and scooped him up into her arms. Cole placed his arm around her, and she leaned into him. The baby sucked on his pacifier while she cried into Cole's shoulder, her soft blond curls brushing up against his neck. Her shampoo's gardenia scent brought back memories, along with powerful feelings for her that he'd thought he'd forgotten. For his own emotional preservation, he mentally pushed them aside once again.

Fifteen minutes later, he led her back to the guest room, where she and the baby could nap. "I'll let you know when dinner is ready."

"I can't eat."

He wasn't surprised. "We'll save you a plate for later."

After closing the door, he found his family gathered around the kitchen island. His mother glanced over at him from where she worked at the stove. "We heard you talking to Sierra. How is she doing?"

"About as well as you might think."

She nodded, her expression sympathetic. "That poor girl has been through so much."

His father tugged open the refrigerator door. "The best thing we can do is continue to offer our support while Cole catches the creep who did this to her sister."

"We'll help with that." Zach turned to Jackson. "Won't we?"

"I'll let my team know I'm taking vacation time." Jackson's stomach rumbled. "But first, I need to eat." Since he was the supervisor of the task force, he had flexibility with his schedule.

"You boys set the table," his mother instructed. "Lily and I will serve."

Cole didn't have time for a leisurely meal. "Mom, I hope you don't mind if I eat at the kitchen nook and work on this case. We're up against the clock."

"I understand." She prepared a bowl of stew and a plate of biscuits while he settled on a bench at the corner table.

He offered a prayer before eating. "Dear Lord, I thank You for this meal." Mindful of his human limitations, Cole added, "I know You have a plan for us. I ask that You guide me down the right path and protect us, especially Sierra and her nephew. Amen."

Cole decided the best use of his time was to figure out where Megan had hid the ledger copies. They could use them as bait. First, he called her friends who still lived in town. They'd already heard about the threats levied against Sierra and were happy to help. He purposely left out the latest news regarding her older sister's demise.

After twenty minutes of asking questions and artfully sidestepping theirs, he had a list of five locations she had frequented during her teens or early twenties. None of her friends had seen her recently. And they weren't surprised she'd left town without paying a visit. Megan had said goodbye to her former life when she moved to Yuma.

Cole looked over the list. A friend's house, bakery, pizzeria, campsite and biker bar. Megan worked as a waitress at the latter for several years, and ownership had never changed hands since opening day. A good place to start. After a quick internet search on his smartphone, he spoke to a deep-voiced man. "This is Detective Cole Walker with—"

He never got the chance to finish his sentence. Aggravated, Cole placed the phone on the table.

"Sounds like someone hung up on you." Sierra stood at the kitchen entryway. She'd run a brush through her hair and added a touch of makeup, but the signs of crying remained. Mainly bloodshot, swollen eyes.

"I'm used to it." He was surprised to see her empty-handed. "Where's Danny?"

"Asleep. Lily volunteered to keep an eye on him." Sierra slipped onto the bench across from him at the table. "Who were you calling?"

He turned the list around and pointed to the last name.

"Oh. Yeah, John won't speak to the police. He mistrusts anyone working for law enforcement or the government."

Surprised she knew so much about the man, Cole furrowed his brow and asked, "Did Megan talk about him?"

"At times, but she didn't need to, since I know him through his daughter. We were in high school choir together."

That was news to Cole. "Would he take a call from you?"

"I don't know why not. What do you want to ask?"

"If he saw Megan when she came to town."

"You think the evidence is at the bar." She accepted the phone after he placed the call. The owner answered on the third ring, and she pushed the speaker function. "John, this is Sierra Lowery."

"You can't fool me. Sierra's in the hospital. It's

all over the news." The call disconnected before she could refute his claim.

The frustration on her face reflected his feelings on the matter. "I'll send one of my brothers over there."

"He won't talk to them, either. If Megan didn't hide her evidence at home, she most likely left it with John." Sierra glanced at the time on his phone and sighed. "I only have thirty-nine hours left to find those papers—if Vogel doesn't try to kidnap me before his deadline. He made a point of warning me not to give the police the papers. My gut says he'll try to kidnap me to get me away from you. We can't waste a second of our time. I have to speak to John in person. There's no other choice."

"I'm not taking you to a biker bar."

"Vogel has to pay for killing my sister." The fierce determination in her voice was unwavering. "If we wait around for the FBI to help, I might be kidnapped and tortured before anyone finds the evidence that will put him behind bars for the rest of his despicable life. Take me to that biker bar, or I'll find someone who will."

FIVE

It was ten o'clock when they parked in front of the biker bar, which looked more like an Old West saloon with its wooden face and hitching post. Neither of them budged from his dark gray truck. The department-issued SUV he used for work was parked at the police station.

"I have to do this. Stop trying to talk me out of it." Sierra's determination pushed her doubts deep down inside. Her gaze collided with Cole's, daring him to argue with her. "This man is not going to get away with killing my sister. Yes, I'm scared to go anywhere Vogel might find me, especially a place known for its brawls, but I won't let fear stop me from taking that monster down."

Cole, resting his hands on the steering wheel, huffed a breath. "The chief might have given his permission for us to come here, but my gut says this is not a good idea."

"I have no choice. I refuse to let a vicious killer raise my nephew. You heard the FBI—if Vogel is arrested now, there isn't enough evidence to put him behind bars for long. I could testify that he broke into my house and attacked me, but a good lawyer can get him off with little time served, and then Vogel would blow up my car with me in it."

"I understand how you feel. I'm just concerned about your safety."

"Me too. That's why I want to find those papers now while you're here to protect me. Not after he's kidnapped me and is holding a gun to my head."

Cole glanced into the rearview mirror. The sheriff's deputy patrolled the area from across the street at the gas station. He would step in if he thought they were in danger.

At least they didn't have to worry about Danny while she spoke to John, the bar's owner. The baby was back at the ranch with Cole's mother, guarded by the Walker family.

"All right. We'll do things your way. For now." He opened his door and stepped out into the night.

She glanced over to the half dozen motorcycles parked in front of a neon sign hanging in the window. When Megan had worked here, stories of smashed bottles and switchblades had made it clear the bikers who frequented this establishment would rather fight than talk. They often proudly shared the stories behind their scars and tattoos.

A shudder reverberated along Sierra's shoulders. If only she were as brave as she'd sounded a minute ago.

Stiffening her resolve, she pushed open her door and slid off the truck's passenger seat. Despite her friendship with the owner's daughter and Megan's close relationship with him while working here for several years, Sierra had never ventured inside.

Cole scanned their surroundings, illuminated by the corner lamppost, then tugged open the front door. "I'll go first."

He'd get no argument from her. Sticking close, she followed in his footsteps. Her gaze first fell on a table where four bearded men sat, wearing black leather vests sporting patches with insignias she couldn't read at a distance. They turned to glare at Cole as if they recognized him. If he had arrested any of them before today, he made no mention of it now.

Two equally intimidating men stepped away from their pool game and gripped their sticks like weapons. The hairs on the back of her neck stood on end. She was just beginning to think she might have made a horrible mistake when a familiar voice called out to her.

"Sierra, I thought you were dying in the hospital." John, the bar owner, strode over and pulled her into a tight embrace. "I'm so relieved you're alive and well."

"I was inside when the bomb exploded," she whispered, despite the bikers remaining too far away to hear their conversation.

John was a New Jersey transplant. His accent was as heavy today as it had been almost two decades ago, when his daughter, Angela, had introduced him to her friends after choir practice.

Sierra noticed the bikers had returned to their conversations and pool game. Megan had once said the rumor that John's brother was a Mafia enforcer back East kept the ruffians here from crossing him or anyone in his circle of family and friends.

John pulled back to study her. "Why did the police chief tell reporters you were in the hospital? And why are you here with a cop?" He glanced at Cole. "Don't bother denying it. I saw your picture in the paper a few months ago. Something about a drug ring."

Cole tilted his head. "I'm not here to cause trouble. I'm helping Sierra."

Sierra touched John's arm to shift his attention back to her. "It's Megan." The horrible truth escaped her lips. "She's dead."

"No." Surprise and regret flickered across his face. "I'm so sorry to hear that. How? Why?"

Unable to say the words, she turned to Cole, who explained, "Megan was murdered in New Orleans."

John's jaw dropped open. "No. She just had a baby. She showed me pictures of him."

"Then Megan did come here last week?" Cole interjected.

"Long enough to fill me in on what she's been doing the past decade." John shook his head. "She didn't say the man she'd left was dangerous, but I could tell by the fear in her eyes."

"His name is Vogel." Disgust rolled off Sierra's tongue. "He's a contract killer. If I don't find the evidence against him, he'll walk away a free man. And he'll take my nephew with him. I need your help, John. Did she ask you to hold any papers for her? She told the FBI that she hid them here in Sedona."

"I'm afraid not."

"Hey, Pops," one of the bikers yelled. "We need another round."

Annoyed, John tossed back, "Give me a minute. I'm busy." He turned to Sierra. "We talked but not about any papers. Looking back on our conversation, though, I can now see she considered it her final visit. She made sure to tell me how much she'd enjoyed working here and that she'd thought of me as a father figure."

"She always did speak fondly of you." All Sierra could give him was a warm smile for his kindness. "Thank you for being there for her when our parents passed."

John held her hands in his. "These papers are important. If you want to look around for them, be my guest."

Cole surveyed the room. "Were you sitting at a table when you talked?"

"The booth over there." John released his grip on Sierra and gestured toward a far corner. "She visited the ladies' room. The only other door down that hall leads to a storage area, but it's locked."

"That wouldn't have kept Megan out," Sierra told Cole with a shrug. "Her sophomore year of high school, she learned to pick our father's home office door when he took her phone away."

John grinned. "Sounds like Megan. Make sure you search the back room." He added for Cole's benefit, "I don't have anything to hide."

His eyes lit up with amusement. "I didn't think you did."

"He's a good guy," Sierra promised John.

"We'll check out the booth where you both talked and let you get back to work."

"I hope you find what you're looking for."

While John attended to his work duties, Cole guided Sierra to the back corner. "Good job."

"It's not like I was up against a dangerous criminal."

"You haven't seen his list of priors," Cole whispered.

Sierra's eyes widened. "He has a—"

"Later." Cole ran his hands under the table and then under one of the bench seats.

Sierra checked under the one on her side, feeling only lumps of gum. "Gross." She wiped her hands on her pants. "Nothing here worth mentioning."

After a quick check of the ladies' room, John let them into a large storage area, where they found boxes on wooden shelves, black aprons hanging on hooks, and a chair in front of a desk covered with notebooks and papers.

"I'll check the shelves," Cole said. "You go through the desk." When she hesitated, he added, "We have John's permission."

"True." The only papers turned out to be inventory lists, bills from suppliers, a check register and payroll documentation. No evidence against Vogel. She ran her hands under the desk and all around each drawer.

When she finished, Cole pulled out the desk and checked behind it. "Not here, either."

She planted her hands on her hips. "Well, this was a waste of time."

"Not at all." Cole lifted her chin with his thumb until she looked directly into his amber eyes. "Each possible hiding place we eliminate from the list leaves us one step closer to the right one."

"I like your optimism." Standing this close to him, feeling the emotional tug between them, reminded her of long walks where they'd shared their hopes and dreams—times best forgotten. He would always be a man walking in death's shadow. "Let's get back to Danny. He probably thinks I deserted him."

They headed down the hall, back to where John stopped wiping down the bar to join them. At the same time, two large men strode inside the front door.

Sierra recognized them from the militia's group picture. She gasped and grabbed on to Cole's arm. *How did they find us?*

The men—wearing cargo pants, military green shirts and menacing scowls—recognized her, too.

Cole pulled her behind him, then placed his hand on the gun holstered at his hip. "Step out of our way, gentlemen."

The one with muscles on top of muscles removed a toothpick from his mouth and tossed it on the tile floor. "If you know what's good for you, you'll stay out of this."

The man with a five-inch scar marring his cheek sneered. "Miss Lowery's presence is requested by a mutual friend. They haven't finished their conversation."

"I'm a police officer," Cole stated clearly. "She's not going anywhere with you."

"I beg to differ." Mr. Muscles reached for his gun, but Cole and the bikers were quicker.

John cocked a shotgun and took aim at Vogel's buddies. "Keep your hands off those weapons, and move away from the door."

Mr. Muscles glared at Cole, his fingers twitching at his side.

Cole's singular goal was to remove Sierra from the premises unharmed. "Don't be a fool. Live long enough to tell Vogel she's sticking to his timeline."

"You're a cop," the scarred guy retorted. "You have to keep whatever she finds."

"No." Cole shook his head. "I won't." That was a partial truth. The FBI would take any evidence—when found. Doubt lingered in their expressions, so he added, "I want Sierra to get custody of the baby without anyone else interfering in any way, at any time." True again.

The bodybuilder rolled his eyes. "I figured you had an angle." His gaze traveled from the armed bar owner to the bikers. If he reached for his pistol, he'd die. Accepting the inevitable, he lifted his hands out to his sides. "Okay. We'll deliver the message."

His buddy raised his hands, and they both stepped away from the door.

John edged closer, with the rifle aimed at the scarred guy, and Cole kept Sierra tucked behind him while they escaped out the front entrance. The second the door closed, he grabbed her hand and ran for his truck. After opening the passenger door, he gestured to the sheriff's deputy across the street to block the pickup wrapped in grassy-camo vinyl.

Cole sped away in record time. While Sierra continually checked her side mirror for anyone tailing them, he called the chief. "There are two militia guys in the biker bar. If you hold them for attempted kidnapping, it will give us time to get back to the ranch."

"Is Miss Lowery all right?"

"Yes, physically. One more thing—the sheriff's deputy is blocking their truck, but he doesn't know why yet."

"I'll tell him and send backup."

The call disconnected, and Cole checked the rearview mirror. So far, they'd made a clean getaway.

He watched the road ahead, the truck's bright lights leading the way. The lack of streetlights outside Sedona made it difficult to scan the surrounding landscape in the dark.

Sierra's silence troubled him.

"You, okay?"

"As well as can be expected. How long until we get back to your place?"

"We have to go back through town first, so it depends on traffic, which shouldn't be bad this time of night."

Minutes later, they entered Sedona, where lampposts and store signs lit the streets. Cars passed them, moving in the opposite direction, but not many.

"No!" Sierra pointed up ahead. "There's a white van up ahead."

It looked like Vogel's vehicle. Cole made a sharp left, sped down two blocks and then made another quick turn. The truck tilted a bit to the side but then righted in time for him to take another corner.

Sierra clung to the grab handle. "Where are you going?"

"As far away from that van as we can get." Back on another main street, Cole searched for someplace to hide. "We need a place where he won't look for us."

She studied the businesses on the passenger side of the truck. "Behind the mini-mart?"

"There might be an alley." Cole drifted into the right lane, then entered the store's small parking area. Two women walked inside, disappearing behind glass doors. Cole drove around back and almost hit a car left between the dumpster and the back exit. The path was blocked. He slammed into Reverse, then drove back to the front side of the store.

Sierra pointed to a white van half a block away. "He's coming! Please do something before he sees us."

Cole darted around to the other side of the building, where the only choice was to dash into the car wash. They didn't have time to enter codes or credit cards. To his relief and amazement, the rollers kicked into gear anyway.

Water cascaded over the truck while Sierra unbuckled her seat belt and turned around. When the soapy pink foam sprayed out at them, she slipped down in her seat. "Vogel's behind us, on the street."

Cole searched for him through the rearview mirror while a faint cherry smell wafted in from outside.

The van traveled slowly. Vogel may or may

not know what they were driving. Cole had to assume the worst-case scenario. Drawn deeper inside the car wash, he tried to map out their location in his mind. There was a side street nearby. He'd have to aim for that. "Buckle back up. Don't worry. He can't see you with the tinting."

Sierra cringed as she returned to an upright position. "Do you think one of your brothers will appear out of nowhere and save us again?"

He gave a half-hearted chuckle. "Highly doubtful. They're watching Danny."

"Right. Exactly where I want them to stay."

Manufactured rain rinsed off the soap before they were tugged into the dryers. Cole made a mental note to pay for the wash if they made it out of this predicament alive.

Before the power dryer shut down, he rolled out of the car wash and searched for any sign of a white vehicle while heading straight for the side street. Two turns later, they were well on their way back to the ranch. Neither of them spoke for twenty minutes.

After they passed the feedstore outside town, Cole knew they were close to home. The stress in his shoulders began to release its death grip on him. "Only a few more minutes."

His headlights bounced off the dips in the road while shadows swayed and flickered beyond both sides of the truck. There were no storefronts or close neighbors from here on— only a dark road leading them to safety.

Sierra appeared to study the darkness out her window, no doubt her thoughts a million miles away—or years in the past. It had to be difficult for her to deal with Megan's death and the real possibility that she was now mother to a three-month-old infant.

His gaze shifted back to the road in time to see a white van blocking the way.

"No!" Sierra grabbed the handhold. "How did he find us?"

Cole didn't have time to respond. He punched the brakes, slammed into Reverse again and sped backward until he could find space to change direction. Mid-turn, he spotted the van advancing on them.

Sierra jolted in her seat. "We have to lose him!"

Cole shifted into Drive and sped forward. Again, he didn't respond. He had to think. Had to come up with a plan. "Call the station. Tell them what's going on."

While Sierra reached for his phone, he raced past the feedstore and back toward town. The distance between vehicles began to grow. The van wasn't built to keep up. There was hope for them yet.

City lights in the distance beckoned them, but Cole dreaded any traffic that could slow them down. He swerved while turning onto an unpaved route. Their wheels kicked up dirt as Sierra rattled off their location to the dispatcher.

The only thing in their favor was Vogel's reluctance to shoot. Sierra was his key to finding those papers, and the guy knew he had to keep her alive—for now.

Seconds later, sirens cut through the night. If they made it to the state road, a quarter mile away, the cruisers could catch up. They bounced over a dip in the road, and Cole hit his head on the ceiling, an annoyance that happened from time to time when you stood over six feet tall. He ignored the dull pain, keeping his eyes glued to what he could see through the dusty haze.

Judging by the few residential lights off in the distance, he guessed they were getting close to their turnoff. Maybe a hundred yards away.

Fifty yards.

Twenty yards.

A vehicle parked in the middle of the intersection flicked on its high beams, obscuring his vision. Cole blinked hard, unsure what to do next.

SIX

Sierra gripped the handhold and held her breath, waiting for Cole to make a move—other than drive straight for the car parked in the middle of the road, blinding them with its headlights. A heartbeat later, the beam dimmed, and flashing blue and red signaled the driver's identity.

Pent-up air rushed out between her lips. They were one step closer to safety. "Our backup's here."

Cole kept his foot pressed to the gas pedal as he glanced in the rearview mirror. "Vogel is retreating."

She turned in her seat to watch Vogel slow, then spin around, kicking up a cloud of dirt. The cruiser took off after him, allowing Cole to steer onto the paved state road, where another cruiser exited to join the chase.

Cole's truck continued to shoot forward at a high speed, telling her they weren't out of the woods yet.

"Do you think Vogel might find a shortcut to head us off again?"

"It's a possibility." He spared her a glance, his expression tight and grim.

"How did they find us tonight? We went through a lot of trouble to keep them from knowing we were staying at the ranch."

"Someone told him about me. I just don't know who, but I will."

Her heart pounded and her arms shivered. Pushing up her sweater sleeves, she felt goose bumps born from fright. Unable to relax, she leaned against the seat, her gaze darting from side to side, searching the dark landscape for trouble until they reached the ranch house.

Inside, she found Mrs. Walker pacing the living room, trying to settle Danny. His whimpering and tearstained face ate at Sierra's conscience. "Here, let me have him." She gathered her nephew into her protective arms.

"I'll call the chief." Cole left the room.

Danny wailed as if admonishing her for leaving him behind. "It's okay," she cooed. "I'm here now."

"He started crying right after you left." Mrs. Walker scrubbed her hand through her blond hair with obvious concern for Danny. "We fed, changed and played with him, but nothing helped. He needed you. You're his anchor now."

"I need him, too." Sierra lifted the baby to her shoulder and patted his back. He began to settle, his cries turning to tiny, feeble sounds until he fell asleep from exhaustion. Instead of putting him down for the night, she thanked Mrs. Walker for babysitting and then carried him to the guest room and eased into the rocker. "I'll always be here for you, little guy."

Cole poked his head inside the opened door. "Is it all right to come in?" When she nodded, he walked over to the small table beside the rocker and set down a glass of water for her. "Can I get you anything else?"

"Thanks, but no. I'm fine." She glanced at Danny. "I shouldn't have left him. Our trip was a total waste of time."

"I wouldn't say that. We've eliminated one hiding place from our list. And now we know Vogel's buddies are in town to help him."

"Speaking of which, did the sheriff's deputy arrest those two at the bar?"

"They're being held for questioning but not supplying many answers."

"Like where Vogel is staying in Sedona?"

"That and a few others." Cole placed his hand on her shoulder. "We'll do everything we can to put Vogel behind bars for the rest of his life."

The alternative would be a nightmare from which she and Danny might never recover.

She held the baby tight against her chest. The pain of potentially losing another loved one—to be raised by a murderer if Vogel took off with him—made her more determined to push aside her fears and fight with all she had for her nephew. "I'll make a few calls in the morning. Maybe we can retrace Megan's steps while she was in town."

"Good idea. It doesn't look like the FBI will get here until tomorrow. In the meantime, we will do most of the investigating ourselves." Cole pushed a stray strand of her hair behind her ear, then kissed the top of her head. "Try to get some sleep. We'll be taking shifts, keeping an eye on the place. We'll wake you if we hear anything."

Sierra nodded, knowing sleep would elude her as long as Vogel was on the loose. How anyone could deal with dangerous criminals on a regular basis was beyond her comprehension. She studied the tall cowboy, who was every bit as kind as he was handsome. "Cole?"

He paused at the door, and his gaze locked on hers.

She was sure she knew the answer to her question, but after spending time together—and her feelings for him resurfacing—she had to hear him say the words aloud. "What we've en-countered recently has me wondering if you've ever thought of leaving law enforcement for a safer career."

His brow furrowed, no doubt remembering why she'd left him in the first place. "No, I haven't. There are people out there, like you, who need protection, and it's my calling to help them."

Sierra could only nod, and the understanding that she'd made the right choice ten years ago hung in the air between them.

After Cole closed the door behind him, she felt a sense of loss. His kiss, a simple gesture she took to convey comfort and support, reminded her of the connection they'd shared. One unlike any other she'd ever experienced.

Rocking back and forth both lulled her to sleep and jarred her awake throughout the night. Danny stirred only once, around six in the morning. She tended to his needs, which included a bottle feeding he practically inhaled, then carried him into the kitchen.

"Good morning." Cole, sitting at the corner table, gestured with his mug toward a pot of coffee warming on the counter. "There's a bottle of vanilla-flavored creamer in the fridge."

The fact that he remembered what she liked after all these years shouldn't have made her smile, but it did. "Thanks. Do you mind holding Danny for a minute?"

"Not at all." Cole pushed his mug out of the way and accepted the baby into his arms. "Danny and I are becoming friends."

While fixing her coffee, she listened to Cole tell her nephew about the horses on the ranch. "One day, you might be a cowboy, too," he stated as if it were a foregone conclusion. "We'll start you out on one of Mom's mares. The one with the best temperament."

Danny babbled his response to that idea.

Sierra chuckled. "As long as he doesn't turn into a bronc rider."

Cole's gaze lifted to hers. "Too risky?"

There was no need for her to affirm his assumption. They both knew her stance on dangerous jobs. "I'll be back in a second."

She returned from the living room with the baby carrier in time to hear Cole's cell phone ring. While he answered the call, she secured Danny in his seat and offered a pacifier to keep him quiet before sitting on the bench beside him. She sipped her coffee, trying not to eavesdrop but failing miserably.

"Will do." Cole ended the call, his eyes clouded with worry.

"What happened now?"

"Do you have a great-aunt named Clara living in Arkansas?"

Sierra hadn't heard that name since she was a teenager. "I only met her once. Why?"

"Clara called the police station when she couldn't reach you." He didn't need to remind Sierra that she broke her cell phone when she threw it against the wall in the chief's office. "Megan spoke to Clara before flying to New Orleans."

When Sierra didn't comment on this surprising new development, he continued, "Clara knew why your sister was making the trip and started listening to the podcast for updates on the judge's murder. This morning, the Cajun Copperhead announced Megan's death on his show and named Vogel as a person of interest."

That familiar sense of dread settled over her again. "I don't want to see what Vogel does next if he finds out about the podcaster."

"You and me both." Cole shook his head and huffed a breath before moving on. "Clara did have good news. I guess you can call it that. Megan told her she didn't take the evidence to New Orleans because she was afraid Vogel would steal the papers before she could give them to the proper authorities."

"That makes sense, although I still don't know why Megan didn't tell me that herself. I was shocked when I heard the ledger and ID copies were still here."

"Your sister didn't want to worry you. Instead, she asked Clara to call you if anything happened to her. Your aunt gave us the clue needed to find the papers."

Sierra arched a brow. "Clue?"

"Clara refused to hear the exact location. That knowledge might put her life in danger, so Megan told her to tell you, 'We always loved sweets.'" He looked at her expectantly.

An expression she returned. "That's all?"

"Do those words mean anything to you?"

"Not much." She wracked her brain for anything her sister had said before leaving that might help. "Megan mentioned she had a craving for cookies. They're sweet, and we both like them. But I know the papers were not in my cookie jar. Vogel or the police would have found them."

He removed the list of possible hiding places from his pocket and marked off the biker bar. "The message starts with the word *we*, so let's focus on places you went together."

"And ate sweets." She glanced at his list. "We never ate dessert at the pizzeria."

"Was there an employee named Candy?"

She smirked. "No, but there was a Bubba."

A smile tugged at Cole's lips as he marked that location off the list. "What about the bakery on Main Street? Did you go there together?"

"We bought doughnuts there with Mom. It's now managed by one of Megan's old boyfriends—Trevor Cartwright. He was probably the only nice guy she ever dated, which is why they didn't last long." The bite of sarcasm Sierra heard in her voice made her cringe. She needed to stop judging her sister for her past mistakes. In the end, she'd died trying to do the right thing.

"I don't remember hearing about Trevor. Do you think he'd cooperate with the police?"

"I can call and ask." An annoying feeling ate at her. "But first, can I use your laptop to check my website?" Her only means of communicating with Vogel was through her blog.

Cole placed the device in front of her, and she typed in her site's internet address. When she found Vogel's threat in the blog's comments section of her website, her jaw fell open. "Oh, no. He must have heard about the podcaster naming him as a suspect."

"What makes you think that?"

"He's moved up my deadline. First, my sister gives me a clue and now he gives me a riddle."

"I guess they were into puzzles. What did Vogel say?"

Sierra read aloud, "'Watch the future king carefully as you cover the board in search of the path to victory, or you'll sacrifice your queen at midnight.'" She suddenly felt light-headed. "I know what *sacrificing the queen* means."

Cole reached over and placed his hand over hers. "Vogel can't write anything incriminating on a public site. *Covering the board in search of the path to victory* is referring to your search for the papers he wants."

"*Watch the future king* is easy. It means to take good care of his son, which I'm doing—but not because he threatened my life. Danny is my nephew."

"The only thing new here is the change in deadline. Now that we know about Megan, he wants out of Sedona, fast."

The vise gripping Sierra's heart refused to relax. Her sister was too young to die. "He's a horrible man. I'd say I was glad he was upset over being named a suspect, but I know what he's capable of doing."

Two distant booms sent her rushing for the back door. Cole grabbed her hand before she got there and guided her toward a window, where it would be safer to search for signs of an explosion. Smoke billowed into the clear sky from the direction of the state road.

She gazed up into Cole's dark eyes, memories of the two critically injured FBI agents sparking an anger in her too strong to suppress. "Who did that monster blow up this time?"

* * *

Cole stood with Sierra at the kitchen window, watching black smoke darken the morning sky. His mother had already come in to check on everyone and returned to the living room with the baby to keep her company.

He wrapped his arm around Sierra's shoulders, hoping to help settle her nerves. They both knew Vogel had to be responsible for the explosion—over ten miles away, by his estimate.

Her breathing grew shallow. "No one is safe in Sedona until those papers are found."

"Let's make sure Vogel doesn't uncover their whereabouts and destroy them." Cole pulled her closer to his side. His gaze traveled to where Zach stood near the barn, facing the direction they did.

"Can you call the chief and find out what happened?" Sierra drifted away, back to the table.

A chill in the morning air filled the space she'd occupied only a moment ago.

"I'm sure his top priority is dealing with the explosion, but I'll leave him a message and ask him to call when he has time." Cole slipped onto the bench seat across from her, his gaze turning at the sound of booted footsteps.

Jackson entered the kitchen, his dark and narrowed eyes conveying his concern. He was staying at the ranch until construction of the new house he would one day share with his future bride, Bailey, was completed. "Is your bomber back at work?"

"He's reminding us he means business," Cole said. "He's moved up Sierra's deadline to midnight."

Jackson poured a mugful of coffee, his mood growing more intense. "I know you don't want to sit here doing nothing while this guy blows up the city, so what's our next move?"

"We have a clue to work with." Sierra's tone held a modicum of hope. "'We always loved sweets.'"

Zach entered the house through the back door, and Cole waited until he joined them to fill both brothers in on Aunt Clara's call to the police station and then added, "Megan hung out at the bakery shop that sells those red-velvet cupcakes Mom likes."

"You want to search the joint," Jackson surmised, leaning against the kitchen counter, mug in hand.

"I'll call the manager." Sierra held out her hand for Cole's phone.

He gave it to her and then turned back to his brothers. "I need to stay here with Sierra and the baby."

Zach removed a carton of orange juice from

the fridge. "Jackson and I can search the place if the manager gives us permission."

"If he refuses, we'd need a search warrant," Cole explained. "The chief won't agree to one. The FBI made it clear that this was their case, but the agents taking over haven't arrived yet. Our actions are limited to anything quick and easy."

Sierra's phone call to the bakery manager was short and productive. She disconnected, then sipped her coffee, keeping them all in suspense. "He heard about Megan's…" Her grim expression told them news of her sister's death had already spread through town. "She did stop by the bakery last week, and he wants to help. Whatever we need."

Zach downed his juice. "Just say the word, and we'll head over there. Jackson knows the best hiding places since he worked for the DEA."

"True," Jackson admitted, "but I usually look for large quantities of drugs. This job is going to require a top-to-bottom search. Do we know how many pages Megan hid?"

"Three. One page was a copy of Vogel's ledger. The other two pages were copies of his phony passports and driver's licenses." Sierra grimaced. "I should go along and help. I've seen the clever places where she hid cigarettes from our parents."

"No." Cole shook his head, adamant she remain at the ranch. "It's not safe. You know what happened when we went to the biker bar. Here, we have my family and the sheriff's deputies to help protect you and Danny. They're guarding the gates, searching the grounds with binoculars and taking turns driving the perimeter. Let's leave this search to my brothers."

Sierra opened her mouth but uttered no sound. The faraway look in her blue eyes was the only indication of the internal struggle she faced before conceding. "You're right. Besides, Danny would cry the whole time we were gone."

Cole knew how hard it would be for her to sit on the sidelines when she wanted Vogel to pay for her sister's death. "There may be a way for you to participate in the search." He gestured toward his phone. "We can hook up with them through a video call. You'll be able to watch their progress and give suggestions."

"Sounds like a fine idea." Zach placed his glass in the sink, preparing to leave.

The stiffness in Sierra's shoulders eased, appearing more content with staying behind.

"All right." Cole stepped away from the table. "I'll call the chief." He hated having to report every move they made like a rookie, but he understood. The stakes were high with a bomber on the loose, and the feds would ask for an update when they arrived.

After a troubling ten-minute conversation, Cole returned to the table. "We have the green light with our plan, but only because the FBI agents heading this way called the station. They're trapped between debris caused by the two bomb blasts."

Sierra's eyes widened.

Jackson gripped the mug with both hands, anger flashing through his expression. "Those agents should check their vehicle for a tracking device."

Cole agreed. "That makes sense. Vogel knew the moment they drove past the first bomb and allowed them to live—this time. But he's highly motivated to keep them away until he has what he came for, so they shouldn't count on him not striking again."

"Even more reason to get moving and find those papers." Zach gestured toward the garage, and Jackson followed, the sound of their boots signaling the path of their departure.

Cole rubbed his chin with the pad of his thumb, contemplating recent events. "Either the FBI has a leak or Vogel has militia friends in Phoenix watching the FBI field office. In that case, he's even more organized than I'd suspected."

Sierra's panic-stricken gaze met his. "I don't stand a chance if he comes after me."

Cole made sure he had her full attention before he spoke. "Don't underestimate the people on your side."

That moment reminded him of when her grandmother had passed away, and he did his best to comfort her. He didn't share any profound thoughts on the matter; he just stuck to her side. All she'd needed was to be near him. The connection they'd shared ran deep—once upon a time.

"I'm sorry," Sierra said, her tone subdued. "I didn't mean to imply you couldn't protect us. It's just Vogel is so…"

"Horrible. I understand." He gave her hand a reassuring squeeze before releasing his grip, tamping down on his memories and the love he'd once felt for her. He couldn't allow the past to interfere with his job. One slipup could cost Sierra and Danny their lives.

If that happened, he would deserve the low-level cases he was relegated to after Detective Gold had been hired to fast track into a supervisory position. That's if guilt and grief didn't swallow Cole up, forcing him to leave the department and his law enforcement career altogether.

Danny's cries jerked him out of his dark thoughts.

"I hate to interrupt." His mother stepped into the kitchen, bouncing the upset baby in her arms. "He wants his aunt."

Aunt. Would Danny come to think of her as his mother? Cole watched Sierra collect her nephew and leave the room.

Cole's mother eyed him knowingly. "Have you eaten anything?"

"Not yet."

"I'll whip up something while you focus on your work. Your father and Lily will be back soon. They'll be famished after tending to the horses."

"Thanks, Mom." He updated his notes, read through the surprisingly thin file on Vogel and gathered his thoughts while the scent of frying bacon wafted toward the table. Cole was disturbed by what little information they had due to the bomber's ability to avoid prison. On the three occasions he was arrested on weapons charges, a talented lawyer had worked the system for his release.

A few minutes later, Cole gave a silent prayer of thanks and began eating breakfast, with Sierra sitting across from him, holding her nephew. His parents and sister ate in the dining room area. This seating arrangement was becoming routine when he worked on important cases.

They were finishing up the last remnants of their meal when Zach finally contacted them. "The manager said he visited with Megan in his office. She was alone in there for at least five minutes. I'll give you two a sweeping scan of the area. If you have any suggestions, let me know."

Cole propped the phone up against his coffee mug, allowing him and Sierra to view the screen. The office contained a wooden desk, leather chair, small plastic trash can, metal file cabinet and a wire shelving unit containing extra supplies.

Off in a corner, Jackson stood on a step stool as he pushed up a ceiling tile. A man Cole presumed to be the manager handed him a flashlight to aid in his search beyond the opening. Soon, disappointment flashed across his face.

Cole scanned the walls he could see through the phone. "Check behind the framed print of strawberry tarts."

Zach complied and only found a wire for easy hanging.

Sierra bounced Danny on her lap and pointed to the screen. "What is that open box on the middle shelf of the wire rack?"

It took several attempts for Zach to find the correct box. "Precut parchment paper."

"If Megan hid the evidence inside the box, she would've folded the papers and planted them in the back behind something that would serve as a distraction, like a reorder form." Sierra's tone held hints of both admiration and irritation. "She was clever. I just wish she had used her smarts to stay clear of men like Vogel."

Cole couldn't agree more.

Zach propped the phone up on the manager's desk, freeing him to search with two hands. When he failed to find the evidence among the sheets of parchment paper, he shifted to the other boxes and plastic containers on the shelves.

Jackson announced that he and the manager were combing through the filing cabinet.

"Not being able to see the whole room is frustrating." Sierra rubbed the stress lines on her forehead before glancing at the wall. "Megan once hid her cigarettes behind an electrical outlet cover in her bedroom. I walked in on her taping them away from the wires."

"On it." Zach asked the manager for a screwdriver.

Sierra explained to Cole, "Megan didn't know I was home that day—not that she'd care either way. I never told on her. Maybe I should have."

"Your sister was breaking rules the whole time I knew her." Cole hated to see Sierra traveling down the road of *what if.* It never led anywhere productive. "I'm confident that if you'd told your parents every time you witnessed her hiding cigarettes, it wouldn't have changed anything other than more arguing between you and Megan."

Her expression said he was probably right.

His brothers examined the inside and outside of everything in the office but came up empty-handed. Finally, they concluded Megan had not left her evidence there, and Cole marked the bakery off his list.

After thanking the manager for his assistance, Zach and Jackson agreed to visit a few of Megan's friends, the ones Cole hadn't been able to contact by phone.

Their father poked his head into the kitchen. "Son, you might want to come see this."

Cole headed in the direction of the living room, concerned by his father's grim tone. Sierra followed close behind, carrying Danny on her hip. The television on the far wall was turned to a local station reporting on breaking news from a helicopter hovering over cars crushed together on either side of two craters in the road. A single black SUV was caught on an island created when sections of the road were destroyed. The banner below the footage read "Three Adults, One Child Injured in Freeway Explosions."

Sierra gasped. "Cole, we have to make this stop."

He was about to agree with her when the phone he was holding dinged with an incoming text. "The chief wants to speak to both of us right away."

SEVEN

Sierra feared what the chief of police had to say. Had they uncovered Vogel's next target? Was there another death?

Her body tensed as she listened to Cole place the call. At least Danny was too young to understand. He sat in his carrier, playing with a toy elephant attached to his pacifier. The kitchen table's bench seating allowed her to keep him close.

"Walker," the chief snapped, his voice carrying through the video call. "Do you have Miss Lowery there with you?"

"Yes, sir." Cole swiveled the screen to show her face.

"Good. This involves you both." He paused briefly, allowing her anxiety to escalate. "I received a midair call from an FBI agent flying in from Louisiana. He'll take the lead on the case until his colleagues are rescued from the bombed-out state road."

Cole glanced in Sierra's direction, his expression pensive. Was he worried this agent would insist on handling the case without any local assistance?

Sierra pressed her lips together, her mind swirling with grim scenarios. What if Vogel blew up this agent's car and she was left alone to protect Danny? How could she prevent a kidnapping? She wanted—no, *needed*—Cole to stay with them.

"The agent's plane lands in thirty minutes." The chief's voice sliced through her thoughts. "He wants a meeting with Miss Lowery in her home. We all believe it's the most likely hiding place for the evidence."

"We only have until midnight and there are a lot more places to search today," Cole said, giving voice to her concerns. They had a plan they were following with the help of his brothers, and this new FBI agent might interfere with their efforts.

"It's the FBI's case." The chief's stone-cold features told them it was pointless to argue. "Since Miss Lowery gave us permission to keep searching her home, I sent over the Flagstaff bomb squad with one of their dogs. The property is clear. And, using the clue your aunt Clara provided, Officer Thomas found a note in a bag of sugar. He's still there at the house."

A note. Sierra gripped Cole's arm. "What did it say?"

The chief read, "'We had fun together.' *Together* was underlined twice. Circling the sentence are tiny drawings of cookies and candy. Does that mean anything to you, Miss Lowery?"

The pictures sounded juvenile—but then, maybe that was another clue. "I assume the note means Megan hid the copies in a place we spent time together as kids, making or eating those specific items."

"We didn't find anything at the bakery," Cole reminded her.

"Let me think." Exhausted and just wanting this whole ordeal over with, Sierra rubbed her forehead, hoping the motion would help draw the answer to the forefront of her brain. "Our mother loved to bake. She gave us homemade cookies at the kitchen table after school. Knowing my sister, she might have drilled a hole in one of the table's wooden legs and stuffed the rolled-up papers inside."

The chief passed on her comment to Officer Thomas through a different phone before he returned to their conversation. "Where else should he look?"

"We have an old plastic playhouse out back. On the weekends, we pretended to bake like

Mom in our toy oven. We placed cookies on a little tray and acted like they were hot when we ate them." She was providing more information than the chief needed, but recounting the past helped her think. "You might want to use a metal detector in the yard, especially around the playhouse, in case she buried the papers in a coffee can. She's hidden all kinds of stuff that way."

Cole's rapt attention prompted her to continue.

"There's a picnic basket in the pantry. When the weather was nice, Mom gave us sandwiches and cookies to share in the yard while sitting on a blanket. Oh! Check between the folds of the extra blankets. There's one on the closet shelf in each bedroom." A blush warmed her cheeks. "I'm sure your officers have already checked them. But do inspect the cloth lining in the basket. Megan could have hidden the papers beneath the thin layer of padding inside the material."

"You're doing great, Miss Lowery. We'll call back if we need your input again. In the meantime, jot down any other ideas you have while you get ready to leave." The chief disconnected the call before either of them could reply.

A knot formed in her stomach. Her home would never be the same. Not after Vogel had attacked her there, and surely not now that she worried over Danny nonstop. If that killer wasn't thrown behind bars for life, he could break in and take his son away any hour of the day or night. Any day. Any year.

Cole's mother entered the kitchen in time to hear part of their conversation. "The sense of smell is powerful. Perhaps the aroma of chocolate will trigger a memory that will help you solve this clue. I could make my cashew clusters."

"I wish we had time." Cole's wistful tone helped ease the letdown. His mother had gone out of her way to help from the moment Sierra and Danny had arrived. "But thanks. I know your clusters would have done wonders to lift our mood. I look forward to them every holiday."

Sierra felt her eyes widen. "Holidays. We ate a ton of cookies and candy every Christmas. And Valentine's."

"Probably birthdays, too," Mrs. Walker added.

Cole placed a pen and a piece of notebook paper in the center of the table. "Megan might have hidden the evidence in a box of holiday decorations."

"*Inside* of decorations or rolled between layers of wrapping paper and shoved back into the tube. She wouldn't make those papers easy to find." The tightness in Sierra's shoulders eased as she began jotting down notes. "Thank you, Mrs. Walker. You've been a big help."

His mother's eyes brightened at the compliment.

Sierra's gaze followed Cole's to the kitchen clock on the stove. So much for beginning to feel better. "We have to leave, don't we?"

Cole's phone pinged with an incoming text. "It's time," he said, stepping away from the table. "Let's gather your bags. Our escort is here."

"No elaborate ruse this time?"

"Vogel knows we're here, and he's bound to have one of his militia guys keeping an eye on the main road leading to your house. We're safer with a police escort."

Anxiety and fear kept Sierra frozen in place. She desperately wanted to stay put, but the clues were connected to her childhood memories. No one else would know which items were related to both her and Megan.

Cole offered his hand. She reached up, needing to lean on his strength to leave the safety of the ranch once again. Their fingers touched, and a warm sensation traveled up her arm to her heart. Her gaze locked on his amber eyes. All she wanted to do was to remain in this home, with this man.

As he helped her up, she looked away and spotted the gun at his side—the weapon he needed for his dangerous job. Like a bubble bursting, the strong feelings she harbored for him retreated deeper inside, where they belonged, replaced once again by gratitude for helping her and Danny.

Cole stepped back to give her room to walk around him. He didn't say anything when he reached over the bench seat to grab the handle of the baby carrier, making her wonder if he had felt anything or recognized the sudden changes in her mood. She couldn't be the only one riding a roller coaster of emotions brought on by their proximity.

Maybe Cole had moved on. And if so? She should be happy for him. He could focus on his work without any distractions.

After gathering her bags, she joined Cole at the back door. Mr. Walker and Lily were both working the ranch, but Mrs. Walker wrapped her in a warm embrace, then brushed a stray strand of hair behind Sierra's ear. "You take care of yourself and the baby. Our prayers are with you both."

"Thank you," Sierra said, forcing the words out past the emotions that threatened to choke her. Leaving Mrs. Walker felt like losing a mother—again.

Cole peered out the window, then pulled open the door and guided her outside while he carried Danny. Vehicles driven by sheriff's deputies guarded their exit. Although Sierra knew they had an escort, the memory of Vogel following them down the dirt road flashed before her. She flinched, then glanced back at Mrs. Walker, hoping God was listening to the kind woman's prayers even if He had stopped listening to hers.

The drive over to her house was tense but uneventful. The first thing she noticed was Cole's department-issued SUV parked out front behind a police cruiser. One of the officers searching her home must have driven it over for him. Her heart fell. He would drive away in it after handing her over to the FBI agent, if that's what the feds wanted.

Her mood spiraled from overwrought to resentful. She felt like a pawn with no say in who she had protecting her. Megan had willingly stepped into this dangerous world, not her. This scenario was why Sierra had fought with Megan over her choice in friends a decade ago. Little good that did.

Needing to feel the baby in her arms, she unbuckled him from his car seat. Danny kicked his legs and stretched his arms out for her. "We're back home, sweetie." She found it difficult to sound pleased when she knew the mess waiting for her inside. Vogel had torn the place apart before the police conducted their search. "Maybe we should sell this house and find a new home. One with only good memories. A new start."

Holding the baby close, she surveyed their surroundings but didn't see anything alarming. Only a few curious neighbors standing outside their houses, watching them and the officer guarding her front door. The sheriff's deputies remained outside while she walked the front path with Cole and Danny.

Embarrassed by the unwanted attention, Sierra entered her home, only to be emotionally knocked off-balance by the immediate memory of Vogel walking out of her kitchen, carrying a coffee mug like he owned the place. Her breath caught in her throat. The broken window glass and pillow stuffing littering the coffee table made the room feel like the attack had happened only minutes ago. Her mind clouded. She couldn't stay here.

Cole watched Sierra stiffen at the sight of her home. He'd worried about bringing her back here. How she would react. Stepping around her, he caught the fear on her face. He set the carrier down on the sofa and reached out for the baby. "Here, let me hold Danny."

She blinked hard, then handed her nephew over. "I'm okay. I was just…"

"I understand." Cole patted the baby's back as he walked. "Let's have a seat." He guided her toward the dining room table, where Officer Thomas sat, combing through a wooden recipe box.

"Find anything?" Sierra directed her question to Officer Thomas as she eased into a chair. A recipe for pumpkin bars, printed on an unfolded piece of copy paper, had been left on the table in front of her.

"Afraid not." The officer stuffed the contents back inside and closed the lid. "I'm glad you two are here. I can use the help."

"It was a good idea to look for the evidence in the box." Cole examined the family surname etched in cursive on the front. "That would have been a good hiding place."

Sierra hooked her thumb in the direction of the china cabinet standing against the dining room wall. "My mother used to keep a bowl of candy beside her crystal glasses. She gave my sister and me a piece when she wanted us to get out of her hair. That fits the clues." She suddenly rolled her eyes and shook her head. "I'm beginning to realize our mother wanted us out of her hair a lot."

Cole had wondered why Mrs. Lowery had

supplied her daughters with so many treats, besides her love of baking.

"We already searched the china cabinet," Officer Thomas stated, maintaining a professional tone at that awkward moment. He then gestured with his head toward Vogel's teddy bear, sitting on the fireplace mantel. "The tech guys were able to redirect the feed to the station. We can keep an eye on anyone entering the house when we're not here. If Miss Lowery approves."

Cole noticed the color had returned to her face. "Sierra, are you okay with a nanny cam in the living room?"

She shrugged. "Fine by me. I wish I'd had one when Vogel broke in yesterday."

Hearing a noise out back, he handed the baby to Sierra and pushed aside the blinds hanging in front of the sliding glass door. An officer out back had dumped a plastic playhouse on its side, most likely checking out the fake oven mentioned earlier. There was no way the large muscular man would have fit through the kid-sized front door. Two yards away, another officer swept the ground with a metal detector.

Sierra sidled up next to Cole and grimaced at the sight of her childhood playhouse on its side. Danny grabbed the blinds, and she took his hand in hers. "Let's play a game. It's called—"

"Boss the Detective Around." He ran his hand

through the baby's blond curls. "Aunt Sierra will carry you around the house, telling the detective—me—where to search for the lost treasure. Where to, first?"

Her nephew had no clue what they were saying but seemed pleased by Cole's attention. She kissed Danny's forehead, then spun on her heels. "Let's go through the Christmas decorations."

"I already checked the wrapping paper," Officer Thomas chimed in. "There wasn't anything stuffed in the rolls or around the ornaments."

"Good to know. We'll take a closer look at the decorations." Cole led the way to the garage, his attention back on Sierra. "I assume you still keep them out here."

"In the cabinets." She followed him outside, carrying Danny on her hip. "You can use Dad's old worktable. It'll make it easier to sort through the boxes."

Once Cole had the first clear storage bin opened on the flat surface, he began removing boxes filled with colorful bulbs, making sure he opened and thoroughly inspected the bottom of each container even if Officer Thomas might have already done so.

"Wait a minute." Sierra held up a clear plastic bag containing a hot glue gun. "I had two spare glue sticks in here last week. They're both gone." When Danny reached for the bag, she placed it down on the table.

"How long was Megan in the house by herself? The longer she was alone, the more creative her hiding place could have been."

"I found her and Danny here after I was gone all day on a photo shoot." Sorrow washed over Sierra's face. "At least we know she might have glued something shut to hide the evidence. That's another clue."

"True." Cole wished he could find the words to erase her pain, but they eluded him. He turned away from her sad eyes and offered a silent prayer: *Lord, please envelop Sierra in Your love. She needs to feel Your comfort during her time of grief.*

Keeping the hot glue gun in mind, he rummaged through the bin for anything that might have been pulled apart and then glued shut. Beneath the smaller boxes of ornaments, he found a ceramic Christmas tree and tipped it over—nothing inside the hole.

Sierra removed a table centerpiece with her free hand while balancing her nephew on her hip with the other. Plastic nutcracker soldiers stood out from the pinecones sprinkled with glitter and fake florals filling a red basket. "You can dismantle this. I never did like it."

"You're sure?" Cole remembered her mother

placing the centerpiece on a table runner and commenting on how the girls had picked it out at a craft fair when Sierra was in kindergarten. That was the Christmas he'd kissed her on the back porch and told her he loved her. "The centerpiece isn't that bad."

She tilted her head and sent him her *you have to be kidding* look. He grinned and made fast work of pulling the decoration apart. The only object hidden inside was the block of green foam that held the plastic flowers in place.

While he pushed the mess aside, Sierra squeezed a Christmas stocking. He didn't hear anything, and she must not have felt anything other than cloth because she set it aside and repeated the process three more times. Once for Megan, their father and mother. Each of them dead. The grief on Sierra's face was palpable.

"This next Christmas, you'll have a stocking for Danny. Plus a ton of gifts. I hope you don't mind if I bring over a few." Cole ran a knuckle over the baby's cheek. "I'll miss this kid after we lock Vogel away. His giggles grow on you."

Cole's chest tightened. He wanted to add that he'd miss her, too, but he couldn't let himself go there. Giving voice to his feelings wouldn't help matters. If he let his guard down and asked her to take him back, she'd only leave—eventually. He couldn't go through that again.

After their search through the entire garage was complete, they returned to the front rooms. He used a step stool to open the air-conditioning vents, then checked beneath furniture and rugs while Sierra tended to her nephew's needs.

The hum of a car's engine jerked his attention toward the front of the house. He peered through the blinds and spotted a man with short brown hair driving up to the curb. The way the guy took his time exiting the sedan told Cole he wasn't one of Vogel's militia buddies—a fact confirmed by the bright FBI letters on the jacket the man shrugged into before heading up the flagstone steps to the officer standing out front.

Conflicting emotions churned in Cole's stomach. Although he welcomed the agent's help, he wasn't ready to step away from his job protecting Sierra and Danny if it came to that.

"Who's there?" Sierra's voice cracked when she spoke from the entrance to the kitchen, where she held Danny.

"The federal agent." Cole did his best not to convey any emotions, even when she frowned.

"It's about time." Officer Thomas crossed the room to open the door and read the credentials flashed in his face. "Welcome, Special Agent Wade Shaw. How was your flight from New Orleans?"

"Long." He stepped over the door's threshold, his features severe. "I assume you're Detective Walker and you're Sierra Lowery." His eyes narrowed at the baby. "And that's the bomber's son."

Sierra flinched at the agent's stern tone. "This is Danny, *my sister's* son. *My* nephew."

Without so much as an apology, the agent scanned the front rooms. "Find anything?"

"No." Cole protectively moved closer to Sierra, feeling the need to act as a buffer. He couldn't just hand her over to this agent, who appeared to have no empathy for her situation. They had to find the evidence now so the FBI would turn their focus to capturing Vogel. She would then be free to stay at the ranch until the bomber was behind bars. "But Megan left two clues for Sierra to find the ledger and ID copies. The hiding place has something to do with sugary sweets, like cookies or candy, and something they did together. We checked the garage, and we're working here now."

"I already checked the front rooms," Officer Thomas announced.

"Since sugary sweets come from the kitchen, Miss Lowery and I will concentrate our efforts there." The agent's long strides covered the living room in no time.

Sierra's glare at Cole made it clear she didn't like the guy and didn't want to be alone with him.

"Detective, I'll start on the bedrooms," Officer Thomas reported.

"Thanks." Cole guided Sierra with a touch to her elbow. "It'll be okay." He hoped. Cabinet doors stood open from previous searches, and the bag of sugar where Officer Thomas had found the second clue sat on the counter near the sink.

"I won't be using this again." Sierra dropped the bag of sugar into the trash can. Appearing agitated, she pushed her hand through her blond hair. "I won't be using anything in the pantry or fridge again."

Cole hated to see her like this. "I'll hire a cleaning crew for you."

She shook her head. "I couldn't accept."

"Can we get to work here?" the agent barked while rummaging through baking sheets.

The FBI agent was rude but right. They needed to find the evidence. And fast.

Danny fussed, and Sierra bounced him in her arms while staring at a picture of kids baking with their mother. Intrigued, Cole removed the framed illustration from the wall and placed it facedown on the counter, with the agent looking over his shoulder.

There was nothing of interest on the back—but then, Cole didn't expect the hiding place to be that obvious. Within seconds, he had removed the backing. Nothing there, either. He noticed Sierra's attention had shifted back to the wall. "What are you thinking?"

"This may sound crazy, but maybe the clue's purpose was to get me thinking about the picture, then the wall I recently painted. There's one place in the garage we didn't search. Megan might have folded the papers, sealed them in an airtight baggie and then hid them inside the can of leftover paint."

Agent Shaw ran out of the kitchen and into the garage. When Cole and Sierra caught up with him, he was already using the screwdriver from the worktable to pry open the can of paint stored in the corner. The lid popped open, and the can tipped over, spilling white paint over the toe of his black boot. He swore beneath his breath and grabbed a rag from the table to wipe off what he could, but it was a hopeless cause. Not bothering to replace the lid, he marched back inside without uttering another word.

Cole huffed an exasperated breath, then secured the lid and used a different rag to wipe the concrete.

"Maybe he's just upset over the bombing of his colleagues." Sierra's tone held sympathy, despite the agent's apparent lack of any for her.

"Maybe. Let's head inside." Cole glanced at

his watch, then up into her worried eyes. "It's almost nine o'clock."

"Only fifteen hours left." Her forehead wrinkled, and her gaze dropped to her nephew.

He placed his hand on her back and guided her into the kitchen.

"I need a breath of fresh air." Sierra carried Danny out onto the back porch and inhaled deeply. "I felt like I was suffocating."

"It is stuffy in there." And Agent Shaw's suppressing attitude only made the environment worse.

The police officer searching the backyard with a metal detector checked his watch, his expression grim. Another reminder they needed to get back to work.

Suddenly, a distant explosion obliterated any sense of calm the town might have had that morning. Sierra shuddered and gasped. Danny cried out.

Cole wrapped his arm around her shoulder, pulling them both close as the dark smoke began billowing into the pale blue sky.

EIGHT

Sierra held Danny tightly in her arms and spun away from the smoky dark mass swallowing the clouds in the otherwise pristine sky. Cole kept his hand on her back as they retreated to the sliding glass door, then stepped aside for her to enter first.

"Vogel must be caught," she said in a low voice, not wanting her anger to upset her nephew.

"I promise I won't stop working this case until Vogel's behind bars, even if I have to do it on my own time. I don't care how many agents the FBI sends this way."

Afraid someone had just died in the explosion, she rested her head against Cole's shoulder and took in the familiar scent of his woodsy cologne. She wanted to close her eyes and float back to years gone by, when they were young and had a lifetime together to look forward to, but she didn't have that luxury.

She stepped back and said, "I knew I could count on you." Her voice broke on spiraling emotions.

"I'll always be here for you, Sierra." He reached for Danny, who went to him willingly, then guided her to the sofa. "Take a minute to gather your thoughts before we get back to work."

The clinking sounds of Agent Shaw rummaging through the kitchen continued. The explosion hadn't derailed his search. Maybe that was a good thing. His gruff demeanor wouldn't help anyone's mood.

Sierra nodded in the agent's direction. "He has single-minded focus."

"You mean he's obsessed, but I get it." Cole sat and bounced Danny on his knee. "I think you're right about Shaw knowing at least one of the agents critically injured in the car bombing."

Sierra lowered her weary body to the sofa and scrubbed her hands over her face as if she could wipe away the horrors of the past day. "When will we know more about…?" She turned to look at the sliding glass door, unable to finish her sentence.

"Soon." Cole swept his gaze over the living room.

Had they forgotten to search anything in this part of the house? Sierra didn't think so.

"Walker." Officer Thomas, radio in hand, gestured for Cole to join him in the hall leading to the bedrooms.

"No secrets," Sierra snapped. "I need to know everything."

Thomas gave a curt nod. "The explosion occurred at the biker bar you were at last night."

Her heart clenched. "No. Not John." Shock and disbelief gripped her like a vise. "Vogel did this because the owner defended us against those militia guys. This is all my fault."

"Don't take the blame for a madman's actions." Cole reached for the phone in his pocket as an incoming call came in. Maintaining his hold on the baby, he checked the caller ID. "It's the chief."

Sierra clasped her hands together, steeling herself for what the man in charge had to say.

"Walker here." Cole listened, his stern expression never wavering. "Okay." He placed the call on speakerphone.

"Good news." The chief's words sparked a glimmer of hope. "No one was in the bar when the bomb went off. John had left ten minutes earlier to make a quick trip to the grocery store, and they weren't open for business yet. Running out of limes saved his life."

Relief rolled off Sierra in waves. She relaxed

against the sofa cushion, then reached over to touch Danny's arm, his sweet face reminding her why she had to remain strong no matter what happened. Officer Thomas smiled before retreating to the back rooms.

"The bomb must have been on a timer," Cole surmised.

"We'll know more later, but that's my assumption." The chief paused. "Vogel will be prepping for his next hit, which could be anywhere."

Sierra sighed. Her respite had been much too short.

"We'll get back to work. There's evidence to find." After the call disconnected, Cole turned to her. "What should we inspect next?"

Police officers were scouring her yard, both front and back. Agent Shaw was combing through the kitchen. And Officer Thomas now worked on the bedrooms after searching the front rooms. Sierra reminded herself that she had been summoned back home because the clues had to do with past times she'd spent with Megan. What was she forgetting?

Her gaze landed on the family photo album among the books piled at the foot of the shelving unit. She retrieved the thick visual history of her childhood and placed it flat on the wooden coffee table. Cole lifted a brow, appearing intrigued by what they might find.

Sierra flipped back the hardcover to find the familiar photographs of her parents' wedding. Seeing the love on their faces, especially during this trying time, brought tears to her eyes. She missed them so much her heart ached.

Danny reached for the pages, and Cole again bounced him on his knee, an obvious distraction. A smile tugged at Sierra's lips when she heard the sound of his tiny giggles. They needed more laughter in their lives. Maybe one day. She returned to the task at hand. The following three pages in the album featured Megan's baby pictures.

Sierra compared the photos to Danny. Mother and son had so much in common at this age: round chubby cheeks, blond curls, bright blue eyes and an innocence Sierra wished Danny could hold on to for all his childhood.

Cole turned the page, urging her on. Soon Sierra located elementary school–aged photos of both her and Megan. The first one featured one of their picnics in the backyard. They each held a chocolate chip cookie while grinning up at the camera. Tears returned to her eyes. *I've missed you, Megan. Why didn't you listen to me? This wouldn't have happened if you had stayed home and stopped hanging around those so-called friends.*

"What did you find?" Agent Shaw's guttural voice jolted Sierra out of her thoughts.

"I'm looking for inspiration." She turned the page. Photographs of the sisters swimming or running through the sprinkler wouldn't help.

Agent Shaw walked over as she came across the section of the album dedicated to their camping trips. Every summer, their father made a game of beating his record time for putting up the family-size tent. Megan's job was working the stopwatch; Mom's job was prepping their meals; and Sierra's job was to divide the marshmallows, chocolate and graham crackers onto paper plates for making s'mores, their favorite sugary treat.

Sierra tapped the picture of her and Megan roasting marshmallows over the campfire. "I wonder if we should search the campsite. Mom always brought bags of cookies and candy. And since Vogel wouldn't know where to find the spot we always reserved, Megan might have considered it a good hiding place."

Cole studied the page. "Is that the same campsite where Megan hung out as a young adult?"

"Yeah," Sierra confirmed. "It's the one on your list."

"What are we still doing here? Let's go." Agent Shaw removed a set of keys from his pocket. "I'll follow you."

Sierra looked to Cole, who shrugged. "Might as well check it out." He handed Danny back to her and stood. "Let's make this a fast trip."

Agent Shaw tugged the door open. "You might want to leave the country if you don't find those ledger copies before Vogel's deadline."

The harsh reminder hit like a punch to the gut, keeping her pinned to the sofa, where she took in a deep, steadying breath. It was bad enough she only had until midnight to find that evidence, but Vogel kept setting off bombs. Were they her punishment for not giving him the copies yet? Or were they a reminder of how vicious he could be to get what he wanted? How many people would lose their lives before this nightmare ended?

Cole shot daggers at the unsympathetic, un-professional agent, who ignored him and exited the house.

Fifteen minutes later, Sierra sat in the back seat of the department-issued SUV next to her nephew while Cole drove. Shaw followed in his rental car, with Officer Thomas behind him in his cruiser.

Sierra continually scanned their surroundings

for any sign of Vogel, hoping they weren't leading him to the evidence. She also didn't want him to know another FBI agent had made it to Sedona. Agent Shaw would become a target. "Take the next left," she instructed.

Cole slowed for a passing car and then turned onto a dirt road winding around bare maple and cottonwood trees. Like their names, the evergreens had maintained their color despite the freezing temperatures a few weeks back. The nearby creek flowed an inch higher than usual with the recent winter rainwater. "Which campsite?"

"You won't miss it. Just keep driving until you can't go any farther." She peered through the windshield, waiting for the cabin on a hill to appear in the distance beyond a copse of pine trees, the first sign they'd reached the campsite.

Her heart lurched when she spotted the familiar surroundings. The possibility that evidence proving Vogel was a murderer could be hidden here now tainted her childhood memories. "This is the place," she said reluctantly.

Cole rolled to a stop in front of a log, blocking further movement. Officer Thomas and Agent Shaw parked on the road's shoulder.

Sierra pushed aside thoughts of the bomber, leaned closer to the front seat and pointed toward the hill. "When Megan was in high school, she used to take the narrow path near our tent to that cabin over there on the neighboring property. Her best friend, Lisa, used to vacation there with her parents. That's why Dad always chose this spot. Our stay was always better if my sister was spending time with her friend."

Outside the SUV, the aroma of pine carried on a chilly breeze skimmed across Sierra's shoulders. She shuddered, then tucked the yellow blanket around her sleeping nephew while Cole took in the setting and announced, "I hope we don't have to dig in front of every tree out here."

She shot him an amused smile, something she rarely did these days. "Megan *never* dug in the dirt. Snow, maybe."

"Did she ever climb trees?"

"Nope. If she wasn't off with Lisa, she was here, usually eating or playing Solitaire."

"What did you do together?" Agent Shaw asked, joining them beside the cars.

"If our parents were busy, we ate cookies and played Go Fish," Sierra answered, carrying Danny toward the empty campsite in a clearing the size of a large living room. "And sang silly songs I don't remember the lyrics to. We never hiked or fished," she added. "We weren't exactly the outdoor type. Dad was."

When they reached the wooden picnic bench, all three men looked underneath, then stood, appearing disappointed.

"You didn't expect it to be that easy, did you?" Sierra walked over to where her father had set up the tent. "If Megan planned to hide her evidence in or near a tree, it would be here."

While the law enforcement officers searched every square foot, she tried to remember everything she had done here with Megan that would fit the clues. Her memories lured her to the campfire pit.

"Something made you smile." Cole's comment caught her off guard as he sidled over to her.

"I was picturing the first time we roasted marshmallows with the special sticks Dad made for us from pieces of unbent wire hanger and wooden dowel rods glued at the ends to serve as handles. They were painted and personalized."

Cole toed a rock near the firepit. "What color was yours?"

"Purple. Megan's was red. The color fit her fiery personality. Even back then, she'd start an argument if I didn't do something her way." If only Sierra could hear her sister yell at her one more time. The sound would be music to her ears. "I remember how mad she got when I tried to sit in her favorite spot by the campfire. She used her new stick to knock my marshmallow into the fire. Mom was *not* happy."

Cole eyed her quizzically. "Megan had a favorite spot?"

"Yeah." Sierra tilted her head and narrowed her gaze. "You don't think…" She moved closer to the circle filled with ash and partially burnt logs. "There used to be a single layer of rock, but Dad was safety conscious and had us help add another layer. Megan left a half-inch space between two to secure her stick when she propped it up at an angle like a fishing pole. She bragged that she could cook her hot dog without using her hands."

Cole crouched in front of the campfire pit and lifted the first rock in Megan's special spot, then the second. The sunlight filtering through the clouds reflected off a metal object lying on the flat surface, where it had been sandwiched between two rocks.

Before either of them could move, Agent Shaw swept in and snatched the silver key. "Looks like it fits a doorknob." He studied Sierra's expression, making the hair on her neck stand. "Was your sister renting a house in Sedona?"

"Rent? No." She looked more closely at the scuffed key. Recognition came to her. "I believe that's the key to the first cabin over there." She gestured toward the nearby vacation homes and rentals.

"Why would she have a key to that place?" Officer Thomas had been so quiet up till now that Sierra had almost forgotten he was there.

"The cabin belongs to her best friend's uncle. Once Megan could drive, she hung out here with Lisa. I heard they'd made a copy of the key so they could steal food and cigarettes from the cabin. Lisa was afraid of getting caught, so I can see her and Megan hiding it here."

Agent Shaw closed his fingers around the key. "You all stay put." The command brought out a Louisiana drawl they hadn't heard before. "I'll check out the cabin."

Cole furrowed his brow. "Without a warrant?"

"You're staying here, so you don't know what I'm doing, do you?" Shaw's harsh tone mirrored his steely, cold eyes.

Cole and Officer Thomas remained quiet. There was nothing they could say that would make a difference.

Shivers radiated down Sierra's back. Once Shaw was out of earshot, she turned to Cole. "I have a bad feeling about that guy."

"I don't trust him." Cole removed his cell phone from his pocket and reported the current situation to the chief. "What do you know about Agent Shaw?" While speaking, he guided her and Danny back toward the SUV.

Officer Thomas stuck close by, silent until the call ended. "What did he say?"

"Shaw had initiated first contact. He knew too much about the case not to be legit, even the names of the agents who were hospitalized after the first explosion here and the ones the FBI rescued from the bombed-out road, so no one made follow-up calls. They will now." Cole opened the SUV's back door for Sierra. "We might be worried over nothing. But until we hear back from the chief, let's head to the house. Thomas, we can use an escort."

"You got it." While jogging to his cruiser, Officer Thomas glanced back toward the cabin as if making sure the agent wasn't outside, watching them leave.

Sierra secured her nephew into his car seat. Her gut told her Agent Shaw was more than just an agent determined to solve a case. What motivated him? She didn't know, and that worried her. He showed no sign of wanting to protect her and Danny.

Cole's gaze bounced between the road ahead and the rearview mirror. Officer Thomas following close behind helped ease his mind—slightly. There was no concrete reason not to trust Wade Shaw. Only a gut feeling fueled by the agent's actions. For instance, why hadn't he spent more time at the house questioning Sierra? The other FBI agents never had time to report to their supervisor before the car bombing, so how did Shaw know enough about the case to gain the chief's trust? Besides knowing names of agents?

It had been five minutes since they'd left the campsite, and a silence thick with doubts filled the SUV. He looked over his shoulder at Sierra, who worried her lip while staring out the window. "You and Danny doing okay back there?"

"As well as can be expected." Sierra was doing better than expected, considering she'd been through more than most people could handle in one lifetime.

When the car signaled an incoming call, Cole pressed the on-screen button. "You're on speaker, Chief."

"Walker, according to the FBI, there is no agent Wade Shaw."

Sierra's gasp from the back seat distracted Cole for a split second. He wanted to provide comforting assurance, but that would have to wait. Instead, he focused on his conversation with the chief. "We'll hightail it back to the ranch. The sheriff's deputies are still there."

"Is the impostor still at the cabin?"

"I believe so, but not for long." Cole's pulse raced. "Officer Thomas is two car lengths behind us."

"I'll send backup to deal with Shaw. Thomas can follow you to the ranch."

The call ended, and Cole checked the rearview mirror. A white compact car trailed the police cruiser well below the posted speed limit. Most likely an innocent driver trying to avoid a speeding ticket. Suddenly, another vehicle came into view, and it looked like Shaw's dark rental car.

Sierra's gaze followed his as she turned in her seat. "He's coming!"

"Let's get out of here." Cole flipped on the SUV's flashing red and blue lights. Thomas did the same. They both sped toward Sedona. The car in the distance accelerated at the same time, pursuing Cole and Thomas, and proving Shaw was the driver.

Traffic was light on the forest road, and anyone they encountered pulled over to the side. Cole's knuckles turned white as he gripped the steering wheel, careful not to lose control of the SUV while navigating the switchbacks.

Coming out of the curve, he glanced in the

rearview mirror and spotted Shaw closing the distance between them.

"He's getting closer," Sierra warned, her voice quivering with fear.

There was no telling what the fake agent intended to do if he caught up with them. Cole floored the gas pedal. Engine roaring, he prayed the SUV would be able to help them escape.

"What can I do?" Sierra leaned closer to the front seat. "Should I call 911?"

"The chief is sending help." Cole caught a glimpse of Shaw pulling up next to the police cruiser. A shot rang out, and Thomas's passenger window exploded. The officer swerved onto the shoulder before veering back onto the road.

Shaw slowed just enough to get a better aim at the cruiser and shot out a back tire. Officer Thomas kept driving. More shots followed, and the cruiser flipped.

"No!" Sierra screamed. Danny cried out.

"Get down! And stay there." Cole wanted to call for an ambulance but couldn't safely release a hand from the wheel, and he didn't want Sierra unbuckling her seat belt to reach up front for his phone. Shaw picked up speed. More cars pulled over as they raced down the road. Hopefully, someone would call 911 to report the rollover.

Through the rearview mirror, he could see Sierra folded over the car seat, shielding Danny with her body.

How had Shaw gotten his hands on FBI credentials? He was most likely taking orders from Vogel and trying to stick close enough to report back any new developments. If his goal had been to kill Sierra, he would have done so at the campsite. Dread formed a knot in Cole's stomach. If either of these guys got their hands on what they wanted, nothing would stop them from putting a slug in her.

"Where's that backup the chief promised?" Sierra's tone sounded more like a plea than a question. Danny continued crying, and her efforts to calm him failed miserably. The baby had to feel the tension in the air. And their excessive speed had to be upsetting him, too.

Cole studied the road ahead, finding no sign of a police presence. *God, we can use some help here, please.*

The fact that Shaw's cover had been blown made him more dangerous. They were still ten miles away from Sedona. If Cole couldn't shake this guy loose soon, he'd have to reduce his speed when they neared the city limits, where the traffic thickened. At a slower speed, Shaw could risk shooting to crash the SUV, causing minimal damage. He would then try to kidnap Sierra and the baby to hand them off to Vogel.

Cole couldn't let that happen. He continued forward, his foot pressed hard against the gas pedal, needing to widen the gap between them. The engine roared and his body tensed as he held on tight, hoping the car could take the abuse.

A white truck suddenly crossed the road in front of them. Cole swerved to avoid a collision. Their SUV flew off the asphalt, over a ditch and plowed into a tree.

NINE

The sound of crunching metal split the cold winter air. The front airbag whooshed open. And Sierra's body buckled with the force of the crash. If it weren't for the seat belt pinning her against the back passenger seat, she would have bounced around like a rag doll.

She stared beyond Cole rubbing his forehead to the evergreen that had damaged the passenger-side hood. In her state of shock, she couldn't hear, couldn't think straight. Her head felt like a shaken snow globe—the pieces of her brain falling back into place speck by tiny speck. She blinked hard, the reality of the situation coming back to her.

Danny. His cries, now audible to her, filled the SUV. She'd tried her best to cover him with her hands, to protect him from injury. A cursory glance showed he was upset but safely secured in his carrier. Tears of gratitude clouded her vision. Feeling His presence for the first time in her life, she broke down crying and prayed, *God, thank You for protecting us, and thank You for letting me know you're here.*

"Sierra, can you hear me? I asked if you two are all right." Cole's voice broke through the first prayer she'd spoken since her parents had died so long ago.

She released her seat belt, her body aching with each move, then pushed aside the baby blanket to check his chubby little arms and legs. "Danny appears to be okay," she reported, wiping away his tears. "Shh. It's okay." Finding his pacifier at his side, she quickly slipped it into his mouth, and the crying ceased. "Everything will be fine."

"What about you? Are you okay?" Cole groaned as he appeared to wrestle with his seat belt release.

"I'm fine. I think. But you sound horrible." She scooted closer to look over his shoulder. Worry for this man took root as she tried to fend off the frightening scenarios wanting to spring to life in her mind. "What's wrong? Are you bleeding? Can you move?"

"I think I sprained my wrist when the airbag deployed." He lifted his arm and grunted. The fact that he hadn't yet turned around in his seat to verify that she and Danny were okay was a bad sign. He might have injured more than his wrist.

"We need to get you to a doctor."

"That'll have to wait," he said, with urgency in his voice as he stared into the rearview mirror. "Look behind you." His clenched jaw and stifled groans told her the degree of pain he was suffering while trying to reach for the gun holstered at his side.

Sierra whipped around in her seat and spotted Shaw exiting the rental car he'd parked along the side of the road. He strode straight for them, gun in hand, eyes narrowed, expression dark and dangerous. Why hadn't they suspected earlier that Shaw was one of Vogel's men and not really an FBI agent?

"No!" She shifted to reach for Danny's carrier, preparing to run if necessary. At the same time, she spotted Cole's injured hand fumbling the gun. She watched in terror as the weapon dropped, hit the SUV's console and fell to the floor in front of the passenger seat. Her heart plummeted, along with her hope of surviving.

Cole lunged across the seat to grab his weapon, and Shaw shot through the driver's-side window.

Sierra gasped. Before she could check on him, Shaw yanked open the back passenger door and grabbed hold of her arm. He pulled her out and held her up in front of his body with one arm wrapped tight around her waist. With a firearm pressed against her temple, he warned, "Don't do anything foolish, or she dies."

She stared through the shattered window, watching Cole return upright in the driver's seat, hands up to show he was unarmed. A momentary sense of relief washed over her. The bullet hadn't hit Cole, but he was still in immediate danger. Nothing was preventing Shaw from shooting at him again. Only this time, he was too close to miss.

Sierra's gaze fell on Danny in the back seat. He started to whimper when she didn't come around to get him. A shudder reverberated across her back. *Shh*, she mouthed, afraid Shaw would kill her nephew if he cried. She had to do something now. "I'll go with you. Just don't hurt anyone," she pleaded to her captor.

Cole shook his head. "Don't, Sierra."

"She's coming with me whether she wants to or not," Shaw growled, pulling her backward to prove his point. "And there's nothing you can do about it."

Sierra had to stop him from killing Cole, the only man she'd ever loved. If anything happened to her, he would ensure Danny was safe and find him a home where he could thrive and be happy.

"I—I think I know where the evidence is," she stammered, trying her best to distract Shaw.

"You think?"

"I'm sure. Positive. We need to go before someone else finds it." She leaned backward, forcing him to take a step. She'd hoped he'd forget about Cole. Instead, her captor turned the gun toward the car, and she shrieked, "I won't help if you kill him!"

"Oh, yes, you will."

He dragged her backward, away from Cole, still using her as a shield. She would have fallen onto the hard ground if he didn't have an arm wrapped around her waist to support her body. Her breathing had grown shallow, and she felt dizzy. What would he do if she fainted?

They reached the other side of the SUV, and Shaw yelled to Cole, "Keep your hands up!"

Shaw pushed her forward, and she realized he planned to take her nephew with them. "No!" Gathering strength from her terror, she dug her fingernails into his arms and her heels into the dirt. "Danny stays here!"

"Knock it off!" Shaw placed the gun at the back of her head, but she didn't care. She would not deliver her sister's baby to that monster.

When he tugged open the back passenger door where the baby's car seat sat, Sierra flew into a blind rage. She tossed her right hand up and back, hitting Shaw's gun hand. The weapon fell behind him.

Cole jumped out of the driver's-side door and tackled Shaw to the ground. Sierra grabbed the baby carrier as fast as she could and ran away, her pulse racing. She had to get Danny away from here.

"Freeze! Or I'll kill him." The voice making her skin crawl came from Shaw.

She slowed, then stopped and turned. He had regained control of the gun and was pointing it at Cole, who held his hands out to his sides, showing he had nothing to defend himself with. If she ran, Cole would die. If she stayed, Cole could die anyway. Her mind raced, trying to find a scenario where they all lived, but her efforts were fruitless.

"Get back here." When she didn't move, he added, "I don't need the brat. Do as I say, or I'll kill the detective *and* the kid."

Sierra shifted the carrier behind her body. She would do anything to protect her nephew.

"I'm losing my patience." He aimed the gun in her direction, then back at Cole.

Sierra's breath caught in her throat. Danny whimpered, and Cole remained frozen in place.

If Shaw thought he could get away with killing the baby, he might be right. This man knew Vogel. She didn't.

She took a hesitant step forward, then another. *God, I know I strayed for so long, but You sent Danny to me for a reason. Please help us again.*

The driver of a red compact car slowed as it approached the accident scene, perhaps preparing to stop and help. Uncertainty and hope flickered through her mind. Shaw turned slightly and shot out the passenger window, then whipped the gun back toward Cole. The car careened forward, the driver escaping with his life, leaving her without any viable choices.

"Move faster!" Shaw ordered, his impatience growing.

She stepped closer and hoped the driver who got away would call the police. Shaw must have thought the same thing. He moved away from Cole, still aiming the gun in his direction. The detective's gaze traveled between her and Shaw as if calculating his next move.

With a look of worry on his face, Shaw closed the distance between them and reached for the carrier.

"You can't have him!" Sierra maintained a death grip on the carrier's handle, refusing to give up her nephew. His tiny cries urged her to fight harder. "I'll go with you. Just let me hold the baby!"

"Let go!" Shaw yanked the carrier away, and she fell, facedown, to the hard ground at his feet.

"Don't hurt him," she moaned, her tears darkening the dirt while her world fell apart. "Give Danny back to me." Hearing the hum of an engine, she lifted her head and spotted Vogel's white van rolling forward. "No…"

Cole held up his hands and took one step backward and then another, his attention focused on the white van as it rolled past Shaw's rental car. Odds of survival were bad enough with one armed man who'd considered him an obstacle to achieving a goal. Now there were two.

God, we need Your help more than ever right now. Please guide me through this situation. While Shaw's attention was drawn toward the road, Cole took cautious steps toward the back of the SUV, where he might be able to duck and run around to grab his Glock off the passenger-side floorboard.

Vogel steered the van onto the shoulder of the road, at least thirty yards ahead of Shaw's rental car, and parked. After exiting his vehicle, the bomber appeared to assess the situation, then strolled closer, stopping short of walking down into the ditch between them. His severe gaze locked on Shaw. "What are you doing with my son?"

"It was the only way I could get the girl to follow directions. She knows where to find the ledger copies." Shaw's stern demeanor broke. He was afraid of Vogel. They all were.

"You plan to take care of her the same way you did her sister?" Vogel's tone held contempt for the man, which confused Cole. Sierra's expression twisted into a mask of horror mixed with confusion.

"Megan tried to get away," Shaw explained, his accent growing thicker.

"She was the mother of my child." Vogel's eyes shot daggers at the man.

"She was a woman who betrayed you."

"Her fate was mine to decide—not yours."

Shaw held the carrier closer to his chest, now using the baby as a shield of protection. "It was an accident. She refused to tell me where she hid the ledger copies, then she fell against the fireplace mantel trying to escape. When I left, she was only unconscious."

"An accident, huh?" Vogel tugged open the back end of his van and reached inside, his actions hidden from view.

Shaw turned his gun on Sierra. "Get up!" he ordered, keeping his voice low. When she paused, he added, "Do you want this kid or not?"

While she pushed to her feet, Cole hunched down and hid behind the SUV, inching closer to the passengerside door.

Shaw handed the carrier to Sierra and shifted behind her, now hiding behind both the woman and the baby, the only people here the bomber might not shoot.

Vogel stepped back, away from the van, holding a flaming Molotov cocktail. He tossed it through the open window of Shaw's rental car.

"What the... Why did you do that?" Shaw demanded; the barrel of his Beretta aimed toward the sky, as if unsure who he should fear most.

Cole used the distraction as cover to pull open the SUV's passenger-side door. He reached in with his left hand and grabbed his Glock. His aim wasn't nearly as good with his nondominant hand, but he wasn't about to go down without a fight.

Vogel aimed at Shaw. "You should have stayed in Louisiana, Gator. You almost killed two FBI agents with all the bombs you're setting off here. I'm not taking the rap for that."

"You should be thanking me. Those bombs have kept the FBI away from you, and the police are dealing with one emergency after another. They don't have the resources to hunt you down or conduct a thorough search for those copies." Shaw pulled Sierra backward, inching her toward the forest. "And if you hadn't documented everything in that ledger, I wouldn't have to worry about getting those copies back. I had to come here to help find them."

Cole clenched his jaw. Shaw was Gator. He was the one who had killed the judge after Vogel taught him how to plant car bombs.

Sierra stared toward Vogel, then at the fire blazing inside the rental car. There wasn't much she could do, caught between two dangerous men equally invested in finding the ledger copies. Cole prayed for guidance again.

"I have everything under control," Vogel swore.

"Right." Shaw pulled Sierra another step back, through a wall of bushes and into a copse of trees. With the foliage hiding his escape route, he pushed Sierra forward and took off running.

Vogel shot into the dense forest where Shaw had fled to. Cole shot at Vogel using his left hand and missed by a few inches, hitting the side of the van instead.

Vogel hightailed it to the driver's side of the van and drove away.

Cole rushed to Sierra, urging her to move quickly toward the street. "We need to get out of here before Shaw comes back for you."

TEN

A fear-induced adrenaline spike propelled Sierra across the two-lane road, away from the burning car and the fake FBI agent hiding in the forest beyond the flames. The rigid frame of the baby carrier slapped against her pant leg. She lifted the handle higher, still rushing her steps. Her bouncing nephew giggled as if it were all a fun game they were playing. Better for him to think that than to know the truth.

She stepped off the asphalt onto the dirt shoulder that sloped down to a patch of grass leading to a wall of bushes and evergreens. Cole motioned for her to walk on his left side, keeping the road to his right. He was shielding her in case Shaw shot at them, and she worried for his safety as well as the baby's. Sirens sounded in the distance, and she released a pent-up breath. Help was finally on the way.

"We need to keep going," Cole warned. "I can carry Danny."

"I've got him. You need to be able to shoot if Shaw comes back." Sierra glanced at the flames reaching out the car window like a caged animal fighting to be set free. She prayed the fire department would arrive soon but not for her sake. For Officer Thomas and to prevent a forest fire. "Will Shaw's car explode?"

"Not likely, but Vogel is a bomber, so I can't be certain."

An added sense of urgency pushed her ahead of Cole, who caught up with his longer strides. He kept his injured wrist close to his side while he kept his nondominant hand hovered near the gun tucked into his waistband. The grimace he wore bore evidence of his constant pain.

The shriek of sirens pierced the air as emergency vehicles sped toward them. Red and blue flashing lights called to her like a beacon. She dug deep for the energy to keep moving toward the first responders who would take them far away from Shaw—wherever he lurked.

Her limbs had become fatigued, especially her arms from the added weight of carrying the baby. Despite her muscles screaming for relief, Sierra refused to slow her steps. Help was near.

Help. Remembering Officer Thomas, she glanced back over her shoulder, hoping to spot him standing near his wrecked cruiser. Her toe hit a rock, and she stumbled. Her stomach lurched. Cole grabbed her arm and kept her and Danny from falling onto the hard ground.

When she regained her footing, she paused to ensure everyone was all right. Danny seemed content, looking toward a flock of birds flying overhead. Cole pressed his lips together, agony apparent in his wide eyes.

"I am so sorry." She wanted to kick herself for being clumsy.

"It's okay. Let's keep going."

Despite his assurances, she felt horrible. He'd endured so much on account of her. Maybe— when the real FBI agents showed up—she should go with them and not look back. A pang in her chest rejected the idea, but she had to be realistic. No matter how much she loved Cole, she couldn't let the past repeat itself. The hurt and rejection on his face when she left him a decade ago was burned into her brain. He needed to fall for a woman who could handle being married to a detective.

Seconds later, a police cruiser pulled off the road twenty feet ahead, and another stopped beside them. When the driver rolled down the window, Sierra yelled and gestured behind her, "Officer Thomas's car flipped back there."

Cole added, "Wade Shaw, that fake FBI agent, fled into the forest behind the car fire. He's armed. Vogel drove toward Flagstaff." The officer reached for the radio to call in the update, then sped away.

"Vogel is long gone, isn't he?" Disappointment slipped into Sierra's tone. Once again, the man who had threatened and attacked her would get away.

"Let's not worry about that now." Cole spoke to the other officer, who insisted he go to the hospital for X-rays. "No need. I know a sprain when I feel one."

The young officer shrugged. "At least let an EMT wrap your wrist."

"If you get us back to the ranch, I'll have someone look at it there."

Sierra didn't ask questions. Neither did the officer. They were soon buckled into the cruiser—Cole up front, her and Danny in the back seat. They only stopped to grab the baby's diaper bag and car seat base out of Cole's wrecked SUV.

On the way to the ranch, Sierra gripped the edge of her seat as she peered through the windows, wondering how long Megan had been kept prisoner before she tried to escape, hit her head and died. Her sister had desperately tried to come back home to her son. Overwhelmed by anger, grief, sorrow and fear, Sierra forced back a tide of tears. The stress in her forehead turned into a pounding headache. *Why, God? Why did You let Megan die?*

While rubbing her temples, Sierra felt Cole's attention turn to her. "You okay?"

"I'm not the one with the sprain. How are you doing?"

"I've had worse," he answered with a shrug. "We'll be at the ranch soon and can rest up. My mother will be glad to see you both."

Sierra turned to her nephew, who had fallen asleep during the ride. It would do them all good to stay somewhere safe, surrounded by caring people. "Danny will enjoy the extra attention. Your mother and sister dote on him."

"As well they should." Cole pointed out a turn to the officer driving and left her alone with her thoughts.

Her mind replayed everything that had occurred after leaving the campsite. Shaw knew his cover had been blown and had most likely turned off his phone. Anyone smart enough to obtain fake FBI credentials and fool law enforcement would know how to cover his tracks.

"Shaw's picture should have been taken by airport security cameras," Sierra noted. "That might help the FBI identify him."

Cole shifted in his seat again. "If he was telling the truth about flying here. He could have driven."

"That's a long drive in a short period of time, and he didn't look tired. I think he flew here right after my sister…" The word *died* couldn't make its way beyond the lump in her throat. She swallowed the thought, then added, "Shaw obviously didn't expect Vogel to get so angry or set his car on fire."

"I noticed that, too. The fact that Vogel still cared about Megan took us all by surprise." Regret flashed over Cole's features. "I'm sorry about your sister."

"Thank you, for your words and for all you've done for Danny and me."

"I'm always here for you," he said, sounding like a friend, but the way he held her gaze conveyed a deeper meaning to his message. They shared an unbreakable bond.

There was so much more she wanted to say, but it wasn't right for her to tell him how much he meant to her when they had no future together. Despair took root in her gut, and she suddenly felt isolated despite the presence of two other adults in the car.

She reached out to touch Danny's hand, reminding herself she still had someone left in her family. Someone besides an elderly aunt in Arkansas, whom she hadn't seen in over twenty years. She needed help greater than any human could provide. *God, please protect us and let Danny stay with me. We've lost so much.*

We need each other. I promise to be a good mother—the best.

The cruiser drove through the ranch's front gate, the sheriff's department vehicles positioned on each side like sentries. When the garage door lifted, her shoulders relaxed for the first time in hours, and she dared to drag in a deep, calming breath.

Once again, Cole's father met them inside the garage. He opened the car door for her. "Welcome back, little lady."

"I wish it were under better circumstances." Sierra waited until he'd removed Danny and the car seat from the police cruiser before she grabbed the diaper bag and headed into the house.

Inside the kitchen, Cole's father narrowed his gaze at him. "What did you do to yourself?"

"The airbag hit my hand when it deployed. It's nothing to worry about—probably a sprain."

"You should know, after falling off the roof and a half dozen horses."

When Sierra raised a brow, Cole was quick to answer, "I was only ten, and Jackson dared me to walk across the roof. And falling off horses comes with growing up on a ranch. They don't enter the world wanting to be saddled."

Mrs. Walker met them in the living room. "The chief called and told us you were headed this way." She took the carrier from her husband and placed it on the sofa. "Sierra, are you all right?"

She nodded. "I'm fine. Cole sprained his wrist."

Mr. Walker patted his son on the back. "Let your mother wrap it up for you and then take some over-the-counter pain medication. You'll be as good as new." Once Cole left the room, he turned to Sierra. "What can I get you?"

"Water would be nice, thank you." She removed Danny from the carrier and relaxed on the sofa, holding him close, wondering if they would ever lead a somewhat-normal life again. She pictured a day when she could sit in her living room and watch him play with blocks or toy cars. Was it too much to ask for?

Sierra pressed a kiss to Danny's soft cheek while still maintaining a tight hold on him. What would happen to them now that two killers wanted her to find the ledger copies?

Cole sat next to Sierra at the dining room table, his wrist secured in a support brace left over from a previous injury. He pulled up her website while she bounced Danny on her knee.

"If I had my phone," she complained, "a notification would pop up on my screen if Vogel left a comment on my blog."

"I know it's not easy being cut off from the outside world, but it's safer for you if he can't track your every move."

"I have the feeling his militia buddies will do that every time we leave the ranch."

"They're no doubt trying. That's why we take so many turns when we go anywhere." When he noticed her home page had appeared on his laptop, he clicked on the link to her blog.

"Anything from Vogel?" Her casual tone was unable to mask her concern. She offered Danny a joyless smile when he patted the table.

Cole scrolled down past Vogel's previous posted comment. "Here we go." His muscles tensed as he readied himself for bad news. He felt like a soldier about to go into battle. In a way, he was. "'You lose an hour for making a mess of things,'" he read aloud.

"What? It's not my fault Shaw's cover was blown. And he attacked us, not the other way around."

"There's more." Cole continued to read, "'And you lose two more hours for shooting at me. Your new deadline is nine o'clock. Be glad I'm leaving you any time at all.'" He could feel Sierra flying into a rage beside him.

"Nine o'clock!" Danny began to fuss, and she patted his back. "I'm sorry, sweetie." She whispered to Cole, "How am I supposed to find those copies in nine hours? We looked everywhere. I'm beginning to suspect she hid them in New Orleans."

If that were the case, they'd never find the evidence in time. Not that they intended to give Vogel what he wanted. The best-case scenario was to use the time he wasn't trying to kill Sierra to find the evidence that would put him away for the rest of his life, then use it to lure him into a trap. If they arrested him too soon, he might not stay locked up for long.

Suddenly, another comment appeared, as if Vogel knew they were reading the blog. "He says a few deputies and a handful of cowboys will not keep you safe. To prove his point, he left you a present."

Her face paled. "What type of present?"

"He didn't say." The hair on Cole's arms stood on end. He slammed the computer shut, worried Vogel might have hacked into the website. The department had access to cyber experts who could look into that. Right now, Cole was more concerned with Sierra's "present."

He jumped up from his seat, snatched his cell phone and marched into the kitchen to where his mother was cooking. "Where is everyone?" His tone came out harsher than he'd intended.

"Your Dad and Lily are exercising the horses. Zach is in town, and Jackson is over at Bailey's house. She's worried about him." Bailey was Jackson's fiancée and had lived through a similar situation not long ago. "What's wrong?"

He lifted his finger to signal his call had gone through. "Chief, Vogel left a threat on Sierra's blog." Cole relayed the specifics, then asked, "Can you get that bomb dog over here?"

"ASAP. And, Walker, watch your back."

When the call ended, Cole heard his mother on her phone insisting his father and sister come home. "I'll call Zach and Jackson, too. They should stay away until we know if there's a…"

Cole gave her a quick hug. "It'll be okay."

"Yes, we'll pray. God will see us through this, too."

Cole knew his mother's faith was strong, but worry lines still creased her forehead. She'd been on this earth long enough to know the road to being "okay" was sometimes rough.

Sierra appeared in the doorway with Danny. "What do you want me to do?"

"Stay away from the windows." He spun back to his mother. "Did the dogs act up today?" Last month, his father brought home two German shepherds to train for ranch work. Their old collie was now deaf and spent most of his days lying in the sun.

"They're puppies. They bark at everything,

especially birds." His mother put on her brave face and led Sierra back to the living room.

His mother was right. The dogs made so much noise no one paid much attention to them. Vogel could have left a bomb anytime after discovering they were staying at the ranch. The fact that he told Sierra about it now meant he knew they were back here.

A minute or two later, Cole was taking the drone out of the garage when he spotted his father and Lily headed his way. Sirens echoed in the distance.

"What's going on?" his father demanded.

"Vogel threatened Sierra." Cole set the aerial surveillance device down on a patch of grass.

"Let me take over," Lily insisted, getting in his way. "I'm the expert flier here."

"You should go inside with Dad."

"No, I shouldn't. You have an injured wing." She took the controller out of his good hand and sent the drone up into the pristine blue sky. "Someone grab my laptop."

Their father slipped inside the house and returned a short time later. He opened the red computer on the small table where their mother sometimes enjoyed her morning coffee.

Cole stepped behind him and watched the live stream of the drone flying overhead. "We're looking for a bomb. He'd want to blow up a structure to make a big production of it."

His father huffed. "I'll walk around the house."

Lily cringed and directed the drone in a new direction. "I really hope he didn't target the stables. We just replaced the one that burned down."

"Let's not go down memory lane." Cole studied the screen, searching for anything out of place, anything that stuck out. The drone flew over Jack, their old collie, sleeping beneath the branches of a tree near the stables.

The puppies yapped and chased after the intruder in the sky. Cole's father whistled, then called for the dogs from the other side of the house, and they took off at the sound of his voice.

"Thank you, Dad," Cole whispered.

Lily chuckled as she directed the drone around the stables. "I don't see anything."

She flew the device higher, covering more ground, and he searched every inch of the screen. He'd almost given up when the sun reflected off a metal object. If it hadn't been for that brief spark of light, he wouldn't have known anything was hiding out of sight.

"The shed. I think I saw something." His nervous energy found release through the tapping of his boot. "Fly toward the door."

Cole's breath caught in his throat when he spotted the bomb.

Sirens drowned out the hum of the drone as the cruisers entered the ranch through the front gate. They'd pass by the shed on the way to the house. "We have to—"

Kaboom!

The ground shook, and he grabbed on to the table, his gaze still locked on the laptop screen. Wood debris flew up at the drone. Then nothing. The screen went blank.

ELEVEN

Sierra paced the living room, holding her nephew against her shoulder while anxiously waiting for Cole to return from the backyard. Finally, he burst through the door, and she rushed over. "What happened? Is everyone all right?"

He began closing window blinds. "Vogel blew up the shed. Debris shattered the window of a police cruiser, but no one was hurt."

"Thank you, Lord," his mother said as she stood at the entrance to the kitchen. "How did this happen? There are sheriff's deputies parked at the gates."

Cole frowned, remembering he'd brought the danger to his home. "I suspect Vogel snuck onto the property late last night, when he was least likely to be caught. And he must have one of his militia buddies watching the roads in and out of here. When they saw we were back, Vogel waited for Sierra to visit her blog—which I'm now convinced he hacked into—then blew up the bomb he planted by the shed."

"He timed the explosion perfectly." Sierra slumped onto the sofa. "He might not have placed a bomb here if I hadn't told him to communicate with me through the blog."

"None of this is your fault." Cole sat on the ottoman and leaned forward to place his good hand on top of hers. "Thanks to you, we have a way to communicate with him instead of always guessing."

"Even if he uses my blog against us?"

"Think of it as a game of chess. His every move is a step closer to his goal of coercing you into giving him the ledger and ID copies when you find them. The alternative is giving them to the police, and he's fully aware that you're spending every minute of the day with a detective. He knows it's a possibility he has to prevent."

"Do you think blowing up your property was a message to you? His way of coercing you into doing what he wants, too?"

Cole gave a reluctant nod. "Yes. And that's why we should leave. Vogel blew up a shed because he didn't want to take the chance he might kill you or his son."

Dread knotted in the pit of her stomach. "If the clock strikes nine o'clock and I haven't produced the papers, Vogel will take drastic action. I fear that will involve me and Danny." Sierra's chest tightened to the point she had trouble breathing. Vogel had to be stopped. The Walkers had generously taken her and Danny into their home, and now this had happened. "Where can we go?"

"Cole," his mother eased onto the sofa beside Sierra. "Can't you stay here and just add more security?"

"Mom, we can't take that chance. Vogel is a professional hit man, and he's proven he can sneak past the deputies."

Mrs. Walker reluctantly gave in, most likely considering the danger to the rest of her family. Sierra worried about them, too. And she feared for Cole's life. "When will the real FBI agents be here?"

"Soon." Cole narrowed his gaze. "If you're afraid I can't protect you—"

"Of course not. I'm worried Vogel will kill you." She wanted to scream the words, to proclaim her love for him, but knew she couldn't go down that road. Not when she couldn't give him more than just words. "He'll want to make sure you're out of the way when he comes after me—whether I have the evidence against him or not."

"I'm not afraid of him. I know Sedona. He

doesn't. And neither do those FBI agents. No one can protect you and Danny as well as I can."

He made a valid point.

"What now?" she asked, glad one of them wasn't afraid of Vogel. The mere thought of him made her shudder.

"We find an empty house." He turned to his mother. "Please call Pearl and ask if she has a rental we can stay in for a few days. One that's insured."

"She'll gladly help any way she can." Mrs. Walker headed toward the kitchen. "I'll give her a call."

"Will it have heat and electricity?" Sierra didn't want Danny to get sick.

"Definitely electricity. We can bring a space heater if necessary." Regret filled Cole's eyes. "I'm sorry we have to move again. I know how hard this must be on you."

"It's hard on all of us, but we'll get through it together." She gazed down at Danny playing with his toes, wishing she could give him a loving home like the Walker family had here.

After Cole left the room to make arrangements for their next safe house, Sierra attended to her nephew's needs. Her stomach churned. Anything could go wrong. This situation wasn't fair to any of them, especially the baby. He was innocent in all this.

She was tucking Danny into the carrier when Mrs. Walker handed her a cup of chamomile tea. "This will help calm your nerves."

The warmth of the cup felt good to the touch. "You're too kind."

"Not at all." She held up her finger, signaling her to wait. "I almost forgot. I have something for the baby." Moments later, she returned with a teething ring attached to a plush toy horse. "Here you go, little guy."

Danny had just started gripping objects, and the cute horse went straight into his mouth. Before long, he would begin teething. Sierra hoped to observe every milestone he reached. "He loves it."

"I wanted him to have something to remember us by." Mrs. Walker eased onto the sofa and ran her finger over the baby's cheek. "Maybe one day you'll bring Danny here for a hayride, and when he's older, Cole can teach him how to ride."

The picture she'd painted brought a tear to Sierra's eye. "That sounds wonderful. Maybe that will all happen…one day."

"Sierra, I know you must feel like your world is falling apart, but you're strong enough to handle this fight. You were a frightened young girl when you lost your parents, but you pressed on, built a thriving business and lived on your own for over a decade. Don't underestimate your strength and that of God. Prayer is your best weapon and comfort."

"Thank you," Sierra whispered, the words barely able to escape the tidal wave of emotions washing over her. "I needed to hear that."

Cole marched into the living room, wearing a baseball cap emblazoned with a coyote, his high school team mascot. "Our ride will be here in a few minutes." He paused to read their faces. "What did I miss?"

"Nothing." His mother stood. "Nothing at all." She headed toward the kitchen. "I'll pack you a cooler full of food."

"Everything okay between you two?" Cole asked Sierra.

"Fine. Your mother gave Danny a horse."

"A…" He caught sight of the teething toy. "Oh, a horse. Cute. For a second there, I thought she gave him a real pony. I wouldn't put it past her." He walked over to the window and peered out through the blinds. Seconds ticked by like minutes.

Sierra sipped her tea, wishing the chamomile would live up to its purported calming qualities. Her shoulders ached with building tension.

"Jackson's here." Cole gathered up their bags, hanging them from the straps over his arm, avoiding the use of his injured hand, then opened the back door and asked, "Any trouble?"

Sierra was surprised to see Cole's brother wearing a white lab coat. Missing was the Stetson he wore everywhere.

"Not at all. Everything's set." Jackson took the cooler from their mother and kissed her on the cheek. "I didn't see anyone watching the gate, but that doesn't mean anything. They could be hiding in the shadows down the road."

"And Doc Taylor?" Cole asked.

"Once I explained the situation, he was fine with loaning us his magnetic sign, plus the clothes. We want to make it look convincing."

Sign? Sierra picked up the handle of the baby carrier and headed to the door. Outside, she spotted a white SUV with a sign, advertising a large animal clinic, clinging to the driver's-side door. Doc Taylor was a veterinarian. "I thought you had a black SUV."

Jackson grinned. "I do. This one belongs to the task force I supervise. Since we investigate militia activities in the area, borrowing it wasn't a problem."

After saying her goodbyes for the second time that day, Sierra jumped into the back seat of their escape vehicle while Jackson secured Danny's car seat.

Cole placed the bags in the back, then slipped

blue scrubs on over his shirt before joining Jackson in the front seat. It would be difficult to see their faces between the dark window tinting, sunglasses and baseball caps.

Mrs. Walker ran out the door, carrying a black hoodie and a pair of sunglasses. She handed them to Jackson, who had already turned over the engine. "These are for Sierra."

Touched, Sierra leaned forward to thank her, then waved as they took off, even if there was little chance Mrs. Walker could still see her. "Where to now? The rental house?"

Cole's movements revealed his continuous surveillance of their surroundings. "We'll need to make a series of turns first to shake off a tail. We'll attract one. I'm positive Vogel's militia buddies are hiding near the ranch."

The mention of a tail made her look around, too. After they were about half a mile away, they passed a fruit stand. A Jeep turned onto the road behind them, and Sierra recognized the bodybuilder on steroids. "We have company. It's Vogel's buddies from the bar. Muscles and Scar."

Jackson turned right at a stop sign, and the Jeep followed. Jackson then turned left. So did the Jeep. Sierra's breath hitched. She stretched across the back seat to place an arm over the baby carrier and prayed for protection.

* * *

Cole leaned closer to the passenger-side mirror, watching the Jeep maintain a three-car-lengths distance between them. They had made no attempt to shield their identity and were clearly following them. Did they assume Sierra was in the SUV, or did they have someone hiding close enough to the house to watch them through binoculars?

Determined to lose their tail, Cole clenched his jaw and held up his phone as a signal to his brother. "Ready?"

"When you are." Jackson gripped the steering wheel and accelerated.

Seconds later, a familiar voice came through the cell phone's speaker function. "Are we doing this?"

"As planned." Cole's serious tone conveyed no second thoughts. This was a go. "We have a Jeep following us."

"I can see you from here." An engine roared through the connection before Joe, his friend since high school, ended the call.

"Hang on!" Jackson warned.

"Okay." Sierra's nervous voice floated up to the front seat.

"We'll be fine." He hoped. Cole peered through the windshield to watch Joe begin driving his hay truck off the feedstore parking lot and onto the road. It paused long enough for Jackson to pass in front of it, then continued toward the trees on the other side, blocking traffic in both directions.

Brakes squealed from behind. Cole grinned, guessing Vogel's buddy must be the driver now blasting the car horn nonstop. Joe inched the truck back and forth as if trying to move out of the way but going nowhere.

Jackson continued driving at a speed faster than the posted limit. "Joe will buy us enough time to make the switch."

"What switch?" Sierra asked, sounding more curious than fearful this time.

"Better to show you than explain the details." Cole shifted in his seat to reassure her with a warm smile. "It would have been nice if we hadn't been followed, but as you can see, we were prepared."

"I admit, I'm impressed." She glanced at her nephew. "Shaking them off was so smooth Danny didn't even wake up."

"We'll try to keep it that way." A half mile up the road, they turned onto a neighboring ranch. Zach waited for them behind a shed with a silver-colored SUV, another vehicle belonging to the Northern Arizona task force. Mud strategically smeared over the back end of both cars should keep anyone from running the plate numbers.

Zach, also wearing sunglasses, jumped out of the driver's seat. "About time you got here."

"We stopped for ice cream," Cole teased and handed his brother his baseball cap, then peeled off his blue scrubs shirt and handed that over, as well. "I don't know if Joe can hold those guys off much longer if they realize they can drive around the feedstore to get back on the road."

"Then let's make this quick." While Zach shrugged on the shirt, Jackson moved Danny and Sierra to the second vehicle.

"Call if you need me." Zach covered his darker hair with the baseball cap.

"Thanks, I will." Cole ran to the driver's side of the second vehicle and checked on Sierra and Danny in the back seat. They both appeared ready to go. He hoped the black tinting on the side and rear windows shielding their identities would help calm her nerves.

Zach climbed into the passenger side of the first vehicle, the one Jackson drove onto the ranch. They exited the main gate, ready to assume the role of decoy.

Cole drove across the ranch to the back exit, where the owner, an older gentleman wearing a rifle strapped across his back, waved before closing the gate behind them. The ranchers in the area all knew and looked out for one another.

Sierra leaned forward in the back seat. "Won't the Jeep follow your brothers?"

"That's the idea. Vogel's buddies will think we're still in that SUV. They'll probably reach Prescott before discovering they've been tricked."

"And that will give us enough time to reach the rental house safely." Sierra blew out a breath that sounded like she was beginning to relax. "You and your brothers must have been great at hide-and-seek when you were kids."

A slight chuckle escaped Cole's lips. "Lily was even better."

They drove in relative silence as they headed down one side street after another, each turn confirming they had not gained another tail. Sierra peered out the windows, most likely keeping an eye out for the Jeep. He did the same.

At the light up ahead, he had no choice but to turn onto the main road in the business district.

"Cole, there's a nursery up ahead where my father used to work. Can we stop there?"

"Why?" He glanced back at her through the rearview mirror. "Does it fit the clues Megan left for you?"

"In a way. My sister and I used to love helping our father transfer flowers to ceramic pots. And the owner used to give us money for the vending machine, so we did eat candy bars there. Megan could have hidden the ledger copies in the back room, where Dad worked."

"It's worth a try, but this has to be a quick stop." Cole found a parking space next to a large truck and scanned their surroundings while Sierra unfastened the baby carrier. He was surprised she wanted to stop instead of heading straight to the rental house. His mother was right about Sierra growing into a strong woman. Maybe she could handle a relationship with a police officer now. *Maybe.*

"This way." Sierra carried the still-sleeping baby inside, with Cole trailing behind. He kept his fingers close to the Glock he'd transferred to the left-handed holster he'd retrieved from the garage before leaving the house.

Cole noticed a redheaded teen clad in jeans and a long-sleeved shirt protected by a green apron assisting a customer closer to the cash registers. They stood beside a row of tables showcasing house plants and colorful flowers kept indoors during the winter. No other voices carried through the room, and the only footsteps he heard were their own.

"That's the owner's grandson." Sierra gestured straight ahead. "The workroom is this way." They both picked up their pace until they reached the outdoor courtyard, where they stopped to scan their surroundings again.

Another enclosed building stood behind rows of cacti, tall plants and tables displaying outdoor flowering plants. Their beauty and mingling scents usually calmed Cole, but he couldn't let his guard down. He squared his shoulders and remained vigilant.

The door of the long shed-type building had a sign that read Employees Only. Cole stepped inside and looked around. A wooden worktable with blue-handled tools sat in the center, surrounded by shelves of pots, more plants in black containers and bags of soil. There was no one to redirect them back to the customer area, so they entered.

"I'll check the higher shelves." Cole dragged over a footstool and began searching beneath pots.

"Run your hands along the flat surfaces. Megan might have taped the papers up there, where no one can see them." Sierra placed the baby carrier down on the concrete floor and looked beneath the wooden table.

"You didn't expect it to be that easy, did you?" Cole smiled while echoing the remark she'd made at the campsite when he'd checked under a picnic bench.

She rolled her eyes. "Funny, ha ha. I see you haven't lost your sense of humor."

"It's always the last to go in my family."

"I do remember that." She pushed a big bag of soil away from the wall and peered behind and beneath. "It must be nice to have a big, caring family."

"I'm blessed," he admitted, feeling horrible over her losing most of the small family she did have. He paused to study her. Sierra's blond curly hair, big blue eyes and gentle nature tugged at his heartstrings. He missed what they once had so much it hurt.

The door suddenly flung open, and fake FBI Agent Shaw stepped inside, weapon drawn.

Cole jumped in front of Sierra.

Sierra lunged toward Danny, but Shaw threatened, "Don't move."

"How'd you find us?" Cole asked, his tone incredulous. They'd been so careful, not leaving anything to chance. No one should have been able to follow them.

Shaw sneered. "This is the twenty-first century."

"What's that supposed to mean?" Sierra glared at him, despite the danger they faced.

"Never mind." He gestured with a wave of the Beretta. "You think the evidence is here—keep searching."

"Why are you so eager to help Vogel get his ledger copies back? He shot at you." Cole kept his hands on the shelves, trying to judge how quickly he could grab a heavy pot. Not faster than a bullet.

"I said, get back to work," Shaw growled. "I want those papers."

Cole realized how damning those ledger copies were for Shaw. "Vogel told you that he didn't just write your nickname on his ledger, right, Gator? He spelled out your real name. That's why you kidnapped Megan to get the pages back. And why you're here, trying to save your own skin."

Shaw charged forward and snatched Danny by the handle of his baby carrier. "Vogel shouldn't have needed my help. He's letting his feelings for this brat get in the way. I won't make that mistake."

TWELVE

"No!" Sierra ran toward her nephew, not thinking, just reacting. When Shaw pointed his gun at her face, she froze. *God, please help me.*

Cole jumped to follow her. His uninjured hand hovered over his holster.

"Don't do anything stupid." Shaw directed his statement to Cole while lowering Danny's carrier to the concrete floor, never once taking his aim off Sierra.

He reached for the ceiling in a show of surrender. "Killing Sierra isn't going to help you find those papers. And you need them as much as Vogel does."

"I don't need this brat." He pointed the gun at her nephew.

Sierra's pulse spiked. "Don't! He's an innocent baby."

"He carries the DNA of a hit man," Shaw sneered the same way Vogel had when he broke into her house. "Killing this kid would be a public service."

"Please don't." Tears streamed down her face. Nothing else mattered more to her than protecting Megan's son. "I'll find the papers." Another promise she might not be able to keep. She could only guess what her sister had done with them.

"Then get to it!" Shaw ordered, still holding the gun on Danny.

Cole took a step forward, capturing Shaw's attention. "She can't concentrate if you keep threatening the baby."

He paused for a moment, then drawled, "Okay, I'll point the gun at you."

Sierra shifted her gaze to Cole, feeling both gratitude and fear for his life. This was a no-win situation, even if she found the papers. Shaw would shoot them once he got what he wanted. They were witnesses. All she could do was buy time.

Shaw removed Cole's weapon from its holster. Sierra held her breath, waiting to see if he would make a move to get it back, but he didn't. Not with her and the baby so close.

Once the fake agent tucked Cole's gun into his waistband, the search of the shelves resumed. Soon, Danny started to wriggle in his seat, opening, then closing his eyes again. Every muscle in her body tightened. What would Shaw do if the baby started crying, making enough noise to draw attention to them? They weren't even supposed to be back here in the workroom.

She held an empty pot in her hands, ready to throw it at Shaw if he tried to harm her nephew. This horrible man was willing to take his anger out on Danny even though nothing was his fault. He wasn't a monster like his father. He was a baby, created by God. If raised by her, she would do her best to see that he grew into a caring young man.

Her nephew turned his face to the side and fell back to sleep. Sierra drew in a deep breath and released it slowly as she placed the pot back on the shelf and continued searching for the evidence that would implicate both Vogel and Shaw in the judge's murder. She remembered seeing *Gator* listed on one of the pages, but was one of the other names his legal identity, as Cole suspected? Was killing the judge Shaw's idea, or was he hired by someone else? If so, was that name listed on the ledger?

Ten minutes later, they had checked the entire workroom and came up empty-handed. Shaw scowled and kicked a bag of potting soil leaning against a table leg. The plastic broke open, and dark dirt poured out over the boot that had already been splattered with white paint back in her garage. He shook his leg and huffed in disgust before pointing the gun at Sierra. "You're coming with me."

Her eyes widened in terror.

Cole held his arm out in front of Sierra and cautiously stepped closer. "Where do you think you're taking her?"

"Back to her house—without you." Shaw's finger closed over the trigger, and he aimed the gun at Cole's forehead.

"Don't be a fool," Cole scoffed. "You show up with the girl and the baby, and the police will follow hostage crisis protocol. If you want to be left alone, you need to take me. They'll do what I say."

"I have a police scanner," Shaw admitted. "They were called away from the house."

"The neighborhood watch is keeping their eyes out for anyone suspicious. You won't be there two minutes before officers are swarming the place."

Shaw furrowed his brow, his beady eyes growing darker. Finally, he relented and waved the gun toward the door. "Both of you, out. Slow and steady. No sudden moves."

Sierra reached for the baby carrier, but Shaw grabbed it first. "I'll take the kid," he growled, giving her no choice.

Biting her tongue, she followed Cole into the

courtyard. Only once did she glance back to see Shaw pointing his gun at her from a five-foot distance. Too close for comfort.

How could this be happening when the sun shined overhead, and the floral plants kissed the air with scents meant to bring comfort? Nothing made sense any longer. Out of the corner of her eye, she caught sight of the owner's grandson. His back was turned to them as he watered tall potted plants from a hose. He was too far away to hear any whispered pleas for help. She wanted to yell but knew better.

Unsure what to do, she kept her steps slow and steady as directed, although she feared the young man might see them and end up collateral damage. Shaw would kill anyone who got in his way.

She suddenly felt a splash on her shoulder and jerked in the direction it came from.

The owner's grandson stood in the middle of the aisle, aiming the hose's high-powered sprayer at Shaw. The water hit him with such force he dropped the baby carrier and held his arms crossed over his face.

Cole lunged on top of Shaw. They both landed on the courtyard's hard concrete floor, where the gun spun away.

Danny wailed. He was wet but not soaked.

Sierra snatched the baby carrier and ran

down the aisle toward the nursery's enclosed storefront. When she reached the glass door, she glanced back and witnessed Cole hitting Shaw with a ceramic garden gnome. It broke over their captor's head, and he fell flat again. She didn't know if she should stay or run.

Danny's cries reminded her they needed to get out of there. It's what Cole would want, too. Besides, it looked like he was winning the fight.

She yelled to the owner's son, "Call the police," then ran, holding the baby carrier in her arms. When she passed an older woman pushing a cart full of flowers, she warned, "Gunman! Get out of here!"

Danny cried harder, and she ached for him. He didn't know why she was shaking him like a rattle. He just wanted it to stop. What he needed was his mommy.

Sierra choked back overwhelming emotions. The automatic front doors opened slowly enough for her to drag in a deep breath. Once they were ajar, a cold breeze swept in, and her spine shivered. With the doors now fully open, she ran to the SUV, the only place she could temporarily hide Danny. She held the carrier by the handle and tried tugging open the car door. Of course it was locked. Why would she think otherwise?

Feeling vulnerable and exposed, she was

about to sit on the asphalt and pull Danny inside her jacket for warmth when she spotted Cole jogging toward them. He was alone—for now.

Danny's cries broke through the steady rhythm of her heart pounding in her ears. She crouched down. "It's okay, sweetie," she cooed while freeing him from the carrier. "Cole is coming. We'll make everything better."

Cole slowed to a stop. "I was worried you might have run straight into the arms of Vogel or one of his buddies." He drew in a deep breath and released it, keeping his good hand near the two guns he'd retrieved—his own and Shaw's— before leaving the courtyard. "He's alive but unconscious. I left him tied up."

Sirens split the air, and relief washed over her so fast that she felt drained and dizzy. She pressed Danny tight against her chest.

Cole stood shoulder to shoulder with Sierra. "Help's on the way." He smiled at Danny, who stopped fussing now that he was being held and reached up with his chubby little hands to touch Cole's chin. "Hey there, little dude."

Leaning against him, Sierra watched a cruiser turn into the parking lot. "I don't know how much more we can take."

"Hang in there." He placed a chaste kiss on the top of her head. "I'm impressed with how amazing you've been throughout this ordeal. Never underestimate yourself."

His opinion mattered to her. How she yearned for a real kiss. One that said *Be mine*. One that promised they could always be together. But that was too much to hope for—and something she didn't deserve, considering their past.

"Just remember this isn't going to last much longer." His tone was softer than usual.

"You're right." She glanced at his watch. "Only seven more hours. Then Vogel will kill me and take Danny if I don't hand over those papers."

Lifting her chin with his thumb, he gazed into her eyes and promised, "That will never happen."

Sierra studied his strong, handsome face, her heart full of love for this good man. He would do anything to stop Vogel and Wade Shaw, but these men were vicious. In the end, they could all die.

The cruiser parked and an officer rushed over to them. "Walker, is everyone here okay?"

Cole nodded, then filled him in on what had happened. Two more cruisers arrived, and while this first officer called for an ambulance, the others entered the nursery, ready for anything.

After Cole unlocked the SUV, Sierra pulled on the door, relieved it opened this time. "Sweet baby boy, let's get you changed into dry clothes."

His return coo brought joy to her weary soul. Danny played with her hair as she grabbed the diaper bag from the floormat and set it down on the back seat.

Soon, a uniformed officer headed straight for them. He wore a grim expression. "Walker, Shaw got away."

"What?" Cole's confusion flashed through his changing expressions. "I knocked him out and tied his hands to a post."

"Either he had help or this guy's some sort of Houdini," the officer stated. "Left to his own devices, he would have had to wake up and manage to get hold of a piece of the broken gnome, probably with his teeth, then saw that cheap garden rope until it frayed."

Cole looked as surprised and upset as Sierra was.

"You have Shaw's gun?" When the officer took it from Cole, he added, "We had trouble getting prints back at Miss Lowery's house. Maybe this will help."

Sierra looked to Cole for an explanation.

"Shaw probably altered his fingertips with a nail file before searching your house. With time, the investigative team will find a clear print."

"Then we'll know who he really is." Sierra removed a dry baby blanket from the diaper bag and draped it over the damp parts of the carrier, then searched the bag for a pacifier. The only small object she came across was a smooth disc she held out to Cole. "What's this?"

"The reason Shaw found us here." Cole's severe tone mirrored his expression. "He must have dropped it into the bag while we were cleaning up the white paint mess he left in your garage."

Sierra's jaw dropped open. "A tracking device?" The thought hadn't occurred to her, but it should have. "Shaw did say we are living in the twenty-first century." She shook her head in dismay. "It seems like everything can be turned into a tracking device or hidden camera."

"That reminds me…" Cole turned to the officer. "Since you know about the lack of fingerprints, do you also know if the chief sent the coverage from the nanny cam in Miss Lowery's house to the FBI in New Orleans?"

The officer shrugged. "Sorry, no."

"Give this to the chief." Cole examined the disc once more before handing it to the uniformed officer. "He can trace it back to the cell phone Shaw is using. He most likely dumped the one he called the station with earlier."

Danny fussed, and Sierra sighed. "I can't find his pacifier. We must have left it at the ranch. The car ride might quiet him down."

When Cole placed a call, she expected it to be

to the chief, but his first words were, "Zach, we need you to find Danny's pacifier and bring it to the safe house. Make sure you're not followed."

Their safe house, one of Pearl's rental properties, turned out to be a newly renovated three-bedroom home on a large lot at the end of a cul-de-sac. Cole guided Sierra and Danny to the side door beneath the carport, where he'd parked the SUV. With each step, he scanned their surroundings, including the sloping hill that led to the main residential street.

The warm temperature inside told him Pearl, his mother's best friend who owned several rental properties in town, most likely had an app-enabled thermostat so she could control the temperature of all her homes remotely. He flipped on the kitchen lights, exposing the shiny new surfaces of the stainless steel appliances and granite-covered island. At least their surroundings would be comfortable.

He locked the door behind them and gestured toward the rest of the house. "This way." They found a cobblestone-colored living room set with indigo blue throw pillows. Sierra eyed the cushions and drooped as if ready to fall asleep standing. He wouldn't blame her if she did. "You and Danny can share the primary bedroom."

Cole headed down the hallway, glancing through each open door until he found the one with an en suite. The queen-size bed covered with a blue comforter would do nicely. He took her small smile as a sign of approval and set down their bags. "I'll be in the living room. Feel free to take a nap. I imagine you can both use one."

"There isn't time." Sierra glanced at the bed with regret in her eyes.

"A short one won't hurt. It might help you remember something that will help us find those papers."

"Maybe."

Cole left her alone with her thoughts and walked back out to the SUV, where he'd left his bag. Groomed shrubs and trees covered the large expanse of red dirt between homes. He paused to study the tallest juniper standing thirty feet away, its trunk thick enough to hide a body. When nothing moved, he scanned the grounds once more, including the road leading up the hill. He texted the chief, asking if an officer serving as their lookout could park near the high school down the main road. He also inquired about the nanny-cam footage from Sierra's house.

Satisfied they were safe for the time being, Cole opened the back end of the SUV. He shrugged the strap of his bag over his shoulder, then tugged the small cooler to his hip and held on to it with his good hand. Back inside the house, he found Sierra sitting on the sofa, her nephew sleeping beside her on a baby blanket she'd spread out for him.

"I couldn't stop worrying long enough to fall asleep."

"Maybe you'll feel better if you just close your eyes for a while." He eased onto the sofa opposite where the baby rested, wrapped his arm around Sierra's shoulder and pulled her close. She leaned against his side, her blond curls tickling his chin. Holding her felt good. Familiar. Warning bells went off in his brain, but he ignored them.

"Cole," she whispered. "I…"

"What?" He pushed stray strands of hair behind her ear.

"I'm sorry for the way I ended things between us. I was terrified you would go to work one day and never come home." She glanced up at him with her deep blue eyes, reminding him of every time they'd sat on a sofa, watching a movie together.

He could get lost looking at her—the way he used to—but he couldn't resist being near her. "You did what you thought was best." He backed up his statement with a gentle squeeze to her hand.

"I was so young and foolish." The regret her words expressed hung heavy in the air between them.

Pushing away the doubt that protected his heart, he admitted, "I heard my mother speaking to you. She's right. You are much stronger now than you were back then."

"Strong enough for us to be together again?"

"If that's what you want." He lifted her chin and pressed his lips to hers, crossing the line that could get him fired. At that moment, he no longer cared about proving his worth to the chief. While he caressed her soft cheek with his thumb, his mind and heart reconnected with the past, and he knew he'd never stopped loving this woman.

The hum of a car engine yanked him out of the kiss. He rushed over to the blinds and noticed a slit he could easily see through—and so could anyone who got close enough to spy on them. He bit his lip, angry he'd let his guard down, and studied the SUV coming down the hill. "It's Zach."

"Cole, before you open the door for him, I need to tell you…"

His gaze locked on hers.

"I want to try to make things work between us."

"Me too." Cole grinned, resisting the urge to kiss her one more time. He knew better. His top priority was to keep them all safe. With that in mind, he checked each blind, ensuring they were all closed. The clack of bootheels hitting concrete outside was his signal to leave the room and open the door for his brother.

"It's about time," Zach complained while carrying in four plastic bags from a local store.

"What's that?" Cole asked, changing the subject.

"I stopped by the store and bought five additional pacifiers, plus more baby stuff, including a travel crib." He hefted his purchases on top of the island. "Did you know a police cruiser is parked near the turnoff to this place?"

"At the high school?"

Zach arched a brow. "Close enough. I thought I was going to get a speeding ticket. She pointed a radar gun straight at me."

"Good. It won't be obvious that she's our lookout." Cole opened a package containing pacifiers and ran one under the faucet, then carried it to the living room, where Sierra was tucking a baby blanket around Danny. His phone rang with an incoming call from the chief.

"I have news," his boss announced in his usual no-nonsense tone.

"Do you want me to put the call on speaker?"

"In a minute." The chief paused before saying, "Good idea on sending the nanny-cam footage to the FBI in New Orleans. This Shaw character is a former agent who left after filing for early retirement five years ago. His real name is Wade Devereux, and his college roommate was the deceased judge's husband. They probably worked together to hire Vogel."

"Why would this guy want his wife dead?"

"Greed. The judge was planning to divorce him."

Cole hazarded a guess. "They had a prenup?"

"He'd leave the marriage with nothing," the chief confirmed. "If she died, he would get everything, including money she'd inherited from her parents."

"I guessed Vogel must have listed this former agent's name in his ledger. Now we know why."

"I asked you not to put the call on speaker because I wanted to spare Miss Lowery more bad news. We have partial video coverage of a man fitting Shaw's description stealing a white vehicle parked near a hiking trail not too far from your ranch. No one has reported it missing yet, so we don't have the make or model. My fear is Shaw followed your brother. The officer near the school reported seeing Zach head to your current location."

Every muscle in Cole's body tightened. "Did she also report seeing that former FBI agent?"

"No, but that doesn't mean he didn't follow Zach, wearing a hat and sunglasses. We're dealing with a man who managed to keep his face from being seen on security cameras and didn't leave fingerprints while searching Miss Lowery's house. He's smart."

"And deadly. Maybe as much as Vogel." A knot twisted in Cole's gut. He glanced in the direction of the living room, wondering how much to tell Sierra and when. "I'll keep my eyes open for these guys."

THIRTEEN

Sierra waited in the living room with Danny sitting in her lap. Cole had been in the kitchen with his brother for a long time. Their muffled voices took on an ominous tone, but she couldn't make out what they were saying. She used to think her fears were worse than reality; then a bomber and fake FBI agent had entered her world. These two fiends were capable of committing crimes her mind wouldn't allow her to imagine.

Cole appeared in the entryway, his expression filled with trepidation. "Shaw might know where we are."

"But we got rid of the GPS device he planted in Danny's diaper bag." The worry churning in her gut for endless hours roiled into ire. "How do they keep finding us? I am so tired of this!"

Danny cried, and Cole walked over to gather him up into his arms. "Everything's okay, little buddy."

She knew nothing was *okay*.

"I'm sorry if I sounded like I'm blaming you. I'm not."

"You're frustrated. So am I." Cole rested her nephew against his shoulder, which calmed his tiny cries. "Hiding isn't easy in Sedona. It's not a big city."

"You're right." She looked into his dark, troubled eyes and could see there was more. "What aren't you telling me?"

Cole hesitated. "According to the FBI, Shaw's real name is Devereux, he's a retired agent and he might have followed Zach here."

Her stomach dropped. "Shouldn't we board the windows or whatever people do before a shoot-out?"

He blinked, then furrowed his brows as if picturing the old Western movies she was referencing. "Double-checking the locks on the windows and then fully closing the blinds is a good idea. I don't think Pearl would appreciate us hacking up her furniture and nailing the pieces to the walls."

"If it comes to it, I think she'd understand," Sierra countered, willing to do anything to keep her nephew safe. "I'll check my bedroom window lock. While I'm there, I'll see if Shaw's in the backyard. The way things have been going for us, Vogel will come here, too."

"I'll go with you." Thinking of the bomber had Cole handing back her nephew before viewing his watch. He then supplied the answer to her unasked question—the one always on her mind. "We have five hours left before we run out of time."

"And because of both these guys, we're stuck hiding here, so I can't even search for the papers." She felt like a mouse trapped between two snakes: one that could be outside and one lurking somewhere in the shadows.

Cole placed his hand gently on her back, leading her toward the hall. "You know you can't give the evidence to Vogel even if you find it, right?"

"I know." She shuddered from raw nerves. "But he needs to think I will. It's the only thing buying us time." She paused at the bedroom door with Danny balanced on her hip. "I was thinking about the bombing that put those FBI agents in the hospital. I doubt there's any real evidence tying it to Shaw."

Cole shook his head. "Nothing a good lawyer can't work around."

"We need those ledger and ID copies. And if we ever find them, I hope the police make quick work of capturing Vogel before he kills me for them."

"I keep telling you, I won't let him touch

you." Cole reached up and cupped her cheek. His touch felt warm and reassuring, if only for a moment. "We aren't going to give up the hunt," he promised, then entered her room to check the window lock. After inspecting the closet and finding it empty, he reported, "You're fine here."

"Thanks. I'm going to attend to Danny while you finish your rounds." She remained silent, watching him walk out her door. If they made it through this ordeal, she wanted a second chance with Cole. Could that really happen?

Danny pulled on her hair.

"Are you trying to tell me something?" After tugging the blond strands free of his grip, she kissed his tiny fingers. "I'll fix you a *b-o-t-t-l-e* in a minute," she said, spelling out the word so he wouldn't start whining.

Since Danny couldn't roll over yet, she placed him in the middle of the bed, then walked over to the window to sneak a peek outside. The late-afternoon sun created shadows, drawing her attention to the patio furniture that appeared to be a recent purchase, along with the small flowering plants and shrubs. A shed, sporting a fresh coat of green paint, nestled in the corner of the wooden backyard fence. She liked the idea that no one could hide behind it.

"Looks like everything is good back here," she told Danny as she made sure no one could see in before collecting the diaper bag. Her nephew was playing with his toes when she pulled out the bottle and held it where he could see. He kicked his feet and reached with both hands, making garbling noises. "I thought you might want this." Although she was still worried, her tone was lighter than it had been a minute earlier. Not seeing anyone out back made her feel better—for now.

She shook the bottle, then fed him while sitting on a padded chair in the corner. All she wanted for this little boy was a life full of joyful moments. He'd always miss his mother, but she was sure he could be happy living with her in their family home, given the chance.

"Sierra." Cole stepped into the bedroom, his strong, handsome looks reminding her of the first time she saw him in her college class so long ago—the first time he'd made her heart skip a beat. "The chief's on speaker," he announced.

Zach leaned against the door frame and offered a slight wave, which she returned, her attention then focused on the call.

"We're all here," Cole said into the phone, holding it high.

"Miss Lowery, the FBI agents from Phoenix who were trapped on the state road have made it to the police station, along with two additional agents. They updated us on their colleagues in the hospital. They'll make a full recovery, as will Detective Gold. I checked on him today."

Sierra blew out a breath. "I am so relieved. Thank you for letting us know." She'd continue to say prayers for them.

"That's not all," the chief said. "The FBI has devised a plan for trapping Vogel."

Fear and hope hit her at once, leaving her light-headed, but then she remembered the immediate threat was the man who might have followed Zach. "And what about the former FBI agent, Shaw or whatever his name is?"

"There's a chance this trap will capture them both. If not, we'll concentrate on finding him next," the chief stated flatly, indicating there was no flexibility in this plan.

"I'm assuming you'll need my help." Her hand had started shaking, along with the bottle. If Vogel figured out this was a trap, he'd go after her—immediately.

"Correct. We'll need your username and password to get into the blog on your website. We plan to post a comment from you, telling Vogel you found what he wanted and left it in a cabin near Flagstaff. We'll also leave directions."

"What if he knows we never drove to a cabin?" Sierra asked, sure her skepticism was written all over her face.

"We'll write back that you sealed the ledger copies in an envelope and had them delivered by someone you trusted."

Her pulse skipped a beat. "He'll assume I mean one of Cole's brothers, and I don't want to put his family in any more danger."

Cole gently touched her arm. "Don't worry about us. Remember, we're all armed."

"Okay… What if he wants to change the location?" She still doubted he'd fall for a trap this simple.

"Again, pretending to be you, we'll write that you've gone into hiding and you're not coming out. He'll have to go to the cabin if he wants those papers."

Cole scratched his chin. This time he voiced his concerns. "We all agreed Vogel probably hacked into the website. He'll know where the post is coming from."

"That's where the FBI comes in handy," the chief shared. "They have savvy tech guys who will handle everything. Vogel won't be able to track where the message originated."

Sierra glanced at Cole and shrugged. "It would make sense for me to insist on a plan where I don't have to risk my life." Finally relenting, she rattled off the information the chief needed, hoping this trap didn't backfire on her and Danny.

* * *

Fifteen minutes after the FBI implemented their plan to trap Vogel, Cole stood beside the front window, peering out through the blinds. There was no sign of danger.

"Not knowing anything is driving me crazy," Sierra complained. Danny played with his horse teething toy while propped up in the corner of the sofa next to her.

Zach leaned against the wall near the kitchen and ran a hand through his dark hair. "No movement out back, and I'm starving. Want something to eat?"

"Mom packed cheese, deli meats and crackers in the cooler." Cole glanced over at Sierra. Dark circles had formed beneath her tired, worried eyes. She needed a good night's sleep.

"Nothing for me." Sierra grimaced, and Zach slipped quietly back into the kitchen. "I hope he wasn't offended. I'm just too nervous to eat. Nervous and…"

"Frustrated," Cole supplied. "Angry. Afraid…"

"All of the above and more." She pressed her fingertips against her forehead, most likely pushing back against a headache. It was no wonder the stress was getting to her; threats coming from two fronts would be a challenge for almost anyone.

"I get it. We all feel the same way." Cole

walked away from the window, convinced no one had followed them to the house. They would have attacked by now.

Sierra needed a shoulder to lean on. He joined her on the sofa and reached for her hand. Her skin felt soft beneath his calloused fingers, the way it did long ago. Did he dare hope they could rebuild what they'd lost? They had been on the road to reconnecting, but the fear on her face now made him doubt it was possible. "You'll get your life back, Sierra. We'll put these guys behind bars."

"How? The way things stand now, there isn't enough evidence to hold Vogel for long. At least there's a stronger case against the former agent." Sierra sighed and let her head fall back against the sofa. "I'm letting Megan down. She trusted me to understand her clues, and I can't come up with any hiding place we didn't already check. I can't focus. Anything could go wrong with this plan to trap Vogel. What if he blows up the cabin and all the law enforcement officers waiting there to arrest him?"

"I'm sure they're consulting with the bomb squad, but we can watch a local channel if it makes you feel any better. An exploding cabin near Flagstaff would be a breaking story." Cole reached for the television remote. "Remember, no news is good news."

Sierra nodded, then touched Danny's feet as if needing to reconnect with Megan's child. "If nothing else, the TV might serve as a distraction."

Zach carried in a paper plate filled with food and three water bottles. "If you don't like cheese and crackers with deli meat, you can wait until dinner. We're having cheese and rolls with deli meat."

"Cute." Cole pointed to the pizza commercial on the television. "The first thing I want to do after all of the arrests is order a large pepperoni."

"With extra cheese." Zach placed the food down, then handed out the water bottles. He took a big swig from the one he kept for himself.

A breaking-news announcement made Cole wonder if the cabin did blow up. The banner at the bottom of the screen read "Car Explosion in Cornville."

Sierra gasped. Cole squeezed her hand, then leaned forward, wanting to hear every word.

A young male reporter stood in front of a field of metal debris. "A witness says he watched a man dressed in a black hoodie drive away from the motel in a white car seconds before it exploded. According to local police, the car was reported stolen earlier today in Sedona. No other details have been released."

"Look!" Sierra rushed toward the television

and pointed to a black boot off to the side of the road near a bush. There was an odd white spot covering the toe area. "That's Shaw's." She wasted no time in returning to Danny's side.

The camera zoomed in closer, as if wanting to capture the personal side of the story. "She's right," Cole told Zach. "Shaw dropped white paint on his boot in Sierra's garage."

"Do you think the bomber blew up this guy because he tried to kidnap his son?" Zach's features twisted into an expression of doubt. "I thought Vogel was some sort of cold-blooded hit man who couldn't care less about his kid."

"That may be true," Cole admitted. "I am sure he considers his kid a possession that Shaw should have left alone. Also, if this isn't a revenge bombing, then it could be his way of silencing Shaw. If arrested, a former agent would know he could leverage information about Vogel to get a plea bargain."

Sierra pressed her lips into a thin line. "I hate for anyone to get hurt…or worse. But I have to admit, I feel better knowing we have one less predator to worry about."

"Let me find out what the police know." Cole wanted further proof of Shaw's death before he'd believe it was true.

While Zach made another round of the house, looking out through windows to make sure they were safe, Cole muted the television and called the chief.

"Walker, any news at your end?"

"We just watched a news report on the car explosion in Cornville." Cole told him about the boot stained with white paint and alerted him to the fact that the call was on speaker.

"I'll see what I can find out," the chief stated. "In the meantime, you might be interested in knowing the bomber's militia buddies are on their way to the cabin. They're still driving the Jeep that followed you."

"Any sign of Vogel?"

"Not yet."

Cole caught the concerned expression on Sierra's face and could almost guess what she might be thinking. "Chief, Vogel might have guessed it's a trap. It's safer for him to send his men."

"We have a Plan B. If they come alone, we'll hang back and jam their cell phones so they can't send pictures of the fake ledger copies. They'll have no choice but to take them to Vogel. And before you ask, we're planting a tracking device on the Jeep."

"Sounds like a well-thought-out plan," Cole admitted. "Please keep us informed." After disconnecting the call, he turned to Sierra. "For now, we wait."

Sierra worried her lip and turned toward the muted television, where images of scorched, white car debris flashed across the screen. "At least we know the former agent didn't follow Zach here."

"But Vogel is still out there. He could be anywhere." Cole pushed to his feet and stretched his stiff legs. "We should find something to cover the cars with as an extra precaution."

Sierra paused from opening her water bottle. "There's a shed out back. Who knows, maybe someone left a tarp in there."

"Thanks for the heads-up." Cole gave her an admiring look on his way to the back door.

"I'm coming with you," Zach said, entering the living room. "There's no sign of Vogel anywhere, and this will go faster with two sets of hands."

They were halfway across the backyard when Cole heard a buzzing noise. "Hear that?"

"Something mechanical. Maybe a power tool or a kid's toy." Zach strode to the wooden fence and peered over.

A drone rose above the neighbor's trees an acre away. Cole tamped down his racing pulse, reminding himself that many people owned drones now, even his family, although theirs was a different size, color and shape.

Zach removed his Stetson and shielded his

face from the device's camera lens as it flew closer. "What now?"

Cole tipped the brim of his hat down over his forehead. "Try to act normal and see what it does."

The drone drew closer, then dove toward Zach, who ducked and snatched a rock out of the dirt yard. He threw it at the device as it flew in a broad curve around the yard. The rock bounced off the side but didn't take it down. At least they'd learned the drone wasn't armed.

They couldn't shoot it with houses in the area, even if they weren't close. When it dove toward Cole, he grabbed a patio chair and swung with his good hand, keeping his injured hand close to his waist. He felt the impact before hearing the smack of metal on metal.

The drone wobbled.

Zach followed up with a larger rock this time. He took out a propeller.

Cole swung again with the chair, and the drone fell into a bush, but the buzzing sound continued.

Zach smashed what remained of the drone with a brick from the backyard firepit. "I doubt any kid is flying this."

"If Vogel's the pilot, he's close." Cole ran back toward the house. "Let's get Sierra and Danny out of here!"

FOURTEEN

After hearing noises out back, Sierra had carried Danny to the bedroom and peeked through the blinds in time to watch Cole and Zach smash a drone. She searched the horizon for the owner, desperately wanting it to be anyone other than Vogel.

She held her nephew close, praying as the brothers ran to the back door and pushed it open with a bang. *God, please whisper in Vogel's ear. It isn't too late for him to fall for the trap.*

"Sierra!" Cole's voice echoed down the hall.

Sierra and Danny met Cole at the door. "I saw the drone through the blinds."

"We can't risk staying here." His firm yet gentle tone conveyed both the severity of the situation and his regret. "Zach's calling Pearl. She might have another empty house available."

She was so tired of running. "You're sure the drone belonged to Vogel?"

"Anyone else would have kept it out of our

reach. I think Vogel saw me through the drone's camera lens, then dived at Zach with the intention of flying low enough to hunt you down while taunting us at the same time."

An image of Vogel glaring at her through the drone flashed through her mind. One knee buckled.

Cole grabbed her upper arm, steadying her and Danny. "I have you."

Despite everything she'd put him through when she broke up with him, he still stuck by her side, no matter how dangerous the situation. "I don't know what I would do without you."

"You're stronger than you think." He lifted her chin with his thumb. "You okay now? We need to leave."

She nodded, not sure she was strong at all. "I'll gather Danny's stuff."

"I've got your bag." Cole strode across the room and shrugged the strap over his shoulder.

Sierra still couldn't believe they were on the run again. No place was safe. She reluctantly returned to the living room and secured Danny in his carrier.

"We're going for a ride." Her voice held a false cheery tone. She was relieved when he didn't fuss. He couldn't be happy about spending more time confined to the carrier. They'd bounced around from one spot to another like a beach ball for the past two days. They both needed some semblance of normalcy.

After tucking the yellow blanket around his little body, she hauled the carrier into the kitchen.

"There's no sign of Vogel out front," Cole said, returning from the driveway to grab two bags from the counter. "We'll need to hurry."

She followed Zach to the door and, with one leg out the door, was about to lift Danny over the threshold when a pop filled the air. Cole jerked and fell against the SUV. The plastic bags fell out of his hands and hit the concrete floor. A can of Pringles potato crisps rolled out, disappearing beneath the vehicle.

"Shooter!" Zach rushed at Sierra.

"No!" she screamed in horror as Cole grabbed hold of the side mirror and Zach pushed her back inside the kitchen.

Two more shots rang out, and metal pinged, followed by the whooshing sound of air. A tire losing air?

"Cole!" Panic squeezed the air out of her lungs. *God, please don't let him die*, she pleaded.

She stood, frozen in place, watching Zach help Cole hobble back into the kitchen. Blood soaked the side of his pant leg.

"I always knew this could happen," she whispered, afraid God might ignore her prayer when she had just started putting her faith in Him again.

"I'll be fine," Cole insisted, grimacing with each move as he limped closer.

Shaking herself out of her fear-induced stupor, she rushed out of their way, placed the baby carrier behind the kitchen island where Danny would be safe, and then ran over to the door to throw the dead bolt into place.

"The shooter's hiding at the top of the hill," Cole grumbled. With his arm hung over his brother's shoulder, he staggered into the dining room. Agony twisted his handsome features, but he didn't complain. "Get me to a chair. I need to call the chief."

Once seated, Zach lifted Cole's foot onto another chair, cut the fabric away with a pocketknife he'd removed from the pocket of his jeans and inspected the entry wound. "It looks like the bullet grazed his leg." He turned to Sierra. "Have you seen any bandages or alcohol?"

"No. This place is a rental property. There's hardly anything here."

"Then grab me some dish towels. One should be wet."

She moved the baby into the dining room, away from the back window, then did as he asked. Staring down at the wound, she fully understood how close she'd come to losing him.

A few inches over, and the bullet would have hit an artery.

Sweat dampened her brow. She turned away and pictured her grandmother's grave, her mother's and father's, and a new one for Megan. There wasn't one for Cole, but there might be one day because of his job, and she couldn't bear the thought.

Why did she think for even one minute that she could build a life with a law enforcement officer? She didn't have it in her to worry about him dying every time he stepped out the door to go to work. She'd known that over a decade ago. Why did it take a bullet for her to remember it today?

Hearing her name through her mental fog, she turned back toward Cole.

"Sierra?" Zach stared at her as if he'd called her name several times. "Hunt for a first-aid kit. I could use some antiseptic wipes, sterile gauze and tape to hold the gauze in place."

Unable to speak, she simply nodded.

Cole was calling the chief when she grabbed Danny, afraid to leave him alone for even a second. This baby was all she had left in the world. She placed the carrier outside the hall bathroom door and flung open the cabinets. Nothing useful there. She repeated her actions in the other bathroom and then the linen closet. "Why didn't Pearl buy a first-aid kit?"

Danny offered no answer. She didn't expect him to.

Sierra had noticed the shooting had stopped after everyone made it back inside. What did that mean? What would happen now? And how long would they have to wait for police backup to arrive?

She couldn't take any more.

Fear and exhaustion consumed her. With tears streaming down her face, she pressed her back against the hallway wall and slid to the floor beside Danny's carrier. She knew she should continue searching for the first-aid kit, but she didn't have it in her to do anything other than sob for at least a full minute or two.

"Your…" She sniffled, refusing to say *dad*. "Vogel must know about the trap," she whispered. "Someone is here to deal with me and take you away."

Danny kicked his foot and spat out a garbled retort.

She peered down at him. "I won't let that happen." Tilting her head, she looked up at the linen closet, and an idea to help Cole came to mind. She choked back her tears, grabbed a sheet from a shelf and carried Danny into the dining room.

Cole touched the handle of his weapon, resting on the table. He locked gazes with her, his eyes bloodshot and weary. "If I pass out, I want you to take this gun. You might need it."

There was no point in arguing. She placed Danny at her feet, unable to summon any encouraging words. They all knew the possible outcomes. Most of them weren't good.

"Your knife, please." She held her hand out to Zach. "I couldn't find a first-aid kit, but I can rip the sheet and tie it around Cole's leg to keep the dish towels in place."

Zach studied her, most likely noticing her tear-streaked face, then handed over the pocketknife. If he thought she had fallen apart, he was right. But when it came to Danny, she couldn't afford to succumb to her emotions for long. She had to take up the slack for Cole.

While Zach left to peer out the bedroom window blinds for the shooter, she cut the fabric at one end and tore off a long strip. "Cole, keep the towels from moving."

He looked at her as if she were some sort of Florence Nightingale. His admiration was misplaced. She was no nurse, not even close. And she knew herself well enough to know this brave front would be short-lived. She wanted to return to her safe, boring life, where bad guys never crossed her path—a life where she never turned on the news and ate ice cream every day before dinner.

"You're doing great, Sierra." Cole grimaced when she tied a knot near his wound. "Now, help me to the front window."

Her stomach flip-flopped. "You could get shot again."

"I'll stay out of the line of fire, I promise." He gestured to a chair. "If you move it next to the window, I can look for Vogel and his buddies."

Understanding his desire to keep them safe despite his injuries, she agreed. After positioning the chair, she returned for Cole but first removed his gun from the table and handed it to him. "Keep your weapon." She held up Zach's pocketknife. "I have this."

His expression told her he hoped she'd never need to wield a knife. He holstered his gun, then reached his good arm around her shoulder. After pushing up to a standing position, he used her shoulder like a crutch and hopped on his good foot.

If he could keep going after all his injuries, she could, too.

Once she got him settled, she peered out the window beside Cole and spotted a police cruiser at the top of the hill. Her heart soared. "Our backup is here."

She was about to run for Zach when Cole grabbed her arm. "Wait a minute."

"Why? We need to tell your brother it's time to go."

Cole separated the blinds just enough to study the cruiser. "I never heard a siren. Did you?"

Her joy fell like a brick. "No. I didn't."

"The chief knows our location was compromised," Cole told Sierra. "The need for immediate help would warrant the use of sirens, and we didn't hear any." He reached into his back pocket for his phone and called the station. A few seconds later, he asked, "Has anyone reported in from this location?"

"Not yet," the lieutenant answered. "We have two responders on the way, but they're not close."

"A cruiser is parked up the hill from our safe house." Cole peered back through the slit in the blinds. "It's sitting in the middle of the road, angled straight for us. I'm concerned Vogel or his buddies might have hijacked it from the patrol officer who was keeping an eye out for us on the main road for us."

"Hold a second." The lieutenant checked, and sure enough, GPS was showing the car belonged to the officer who had been parked near the school, and she wasn't answering her radio.

"Backup is five miles away. I'll call the chief," he stated before disconnecting.

Sierra stood at the other end of the window, sending him a questioning glance. Danny was tucked safely away in his carrier, up against the wall.

"It looks like we're in for a showdown." Cole placed his Glock on the windowsill, ready to use, and turned to yell for his brother. "Zach!"

"Detective," the unexpected, deep voice crackled over the cruiser's public address system outside. "I know you can hear me. Send out the girl."

Sierra's eyes widened. "That's Vogel. I will *never* forget that voice."

Cole locked on her gaze, imploring her to trust him. He loved Sierra and was willing to die for her even though he feared this gunshot to his leg may have scared her off for good. He wouldn't blame her if she decided not to give their relationship a second chance. He could've died today.

The fear reflected in her features intensified. "He'll—"

Zach came rushing in from the bedrooms. "What do you want me to do?"

"Take Sierra and Danny into the hall. Keep them there until I tell you otherwise." Cole peered out at the cruiser, still sitting there like it was challenging them. He scanned the cul-de-sac, assessing the possible collateral damage if Vogel started shooting. There were two other houses on oversize lots, one on each side of Pearl's rental property. No one had stepped outside either home to see where the voice had come from. The residents were most likely away, but with dinnertime approaching, they might come back.

A sidelong glance confirmed Sierra and Danny were waiting in the hall, well away from the line of fire. Zach kept her in place with a hand to her shoulder. She closed her eyes and mumbled words he couldn't hear, maybe a prayer. Good idea.

God, I believe You sent Sierra and her nephew to me for help. I need Your guidance now if I'm to keep them alive.

Cole ducked low and reached to unlock the window and slide it open. He needed time to come up with a plan. When no shots fired into the living room, he leaned against the wall and separated the blinds enough to be heard clearly. "Let's talk!"

"Let's not," Vogel countered. "The girl's mine. She set me up."

"If anyone set you up, it's the FBI. You tried to bomb their agents—twice."

"That was Gator," Vogel bellowed over the

loudspeaker. "I didn't set off any of the bombs here, and I didn't supply them, either."

He's sticking to his story. A long pause followed, and the car stayed still. Dread settled in Cole's gut, so he went out on a limb, hoping his idea didn't backfire. "Let's make a trade. I have the ledger and ID copies."

Sierra shook her head vehemently.

"I don't believe you," Vogel snapped back.

Cole turned to Sierra. "Tell me something I would only know if I had the copies."

She rubbed her forehead for several long seconds. "Megan said he documented five jobs in red, boxed letters. He wrote down dates, names, bank account numbers and how much he was paid under each alias. Gator was on the list."

"That might work." Cole released a slow breath, his mind racing. "Did either of you see white paper in this place? Something that might fool him?"

"In a kitchen drawer." Zach strode out of the hallway. "Pearl left behind inventory lists and instructions for her contractor. How many pages do you need?"

"Three," Sierra supplied.

Zach returned a short time later. Cole punched out the screen and waved the papers out the window like a white flag, only he wasn't surrendering. He then repeated what Sierra said was on the ledger and hoped the physical pages would serve as a distraction. They didn't need Vogel asking direct questions.

"Vogel," Cole shouted. "I'll trade this evidence against you for the safe exit of three people, including your son."

"Four," Sierra urged. "There are four of us."

"I have to stay here to keep him from going after you." Cole stiffened his back, locking his feelings away where they couldn't interfere with his job. He knew he might not survive this day. Vogel wasn't about to walk over to the window to collect the evidence against him.

Cole hated to admit it, but Sierra had been right to break up with him when his career in law enforcement was just beginning.

"You're coming with us," Sierra demanded, pleading with her wide, sad eyes.

The PA system squawked. "How do I know you didn't already send a picture of the evidence to the police?"

"You can check for yourself." Cole dropped his phone out the window. He heard it land with a thump on the red dirt below. "Besides, a good lawyer can get a copy of a copy dismissed in court." Maybe.

Another long pause followed before Vogel replied, "Okay, they have two minutes to get out of there."

"We're not leaving you," Sierra stated emphatically as Zach picked up the baby carrier and guided her out of the hall and through the living room.

"We have no other choice." Cole hated not being able to walk. He wanted to pull her into his arms and kiss her goodbye. The pain of his heart tearing apart hurt much more than the gunshot. "Zach, take Sierra out the back door. Run to one of the neighbors behind us, not on the sides. It doesn't look like they're home. I'll buy you as much time as I can."

Sierra tugged on Zach's arm. "He's your brother, don't leave him here. You can throw him over your shoulder and carry him out."

"He knows what's best," Zach argued, not letting her slow him down. Before exiting the room, he turned to his brother. "I'll find a clear shot at Vogel."

"Their safety comes first." Cole's tone held no room for argument. "Promise me."

"I promise." Zach hesitated long enough to exchange one last look of brotherly concern.

"Don't you dare die on me, Cole Walker." Sierra's voice wobbled and broke. "I'll never forgive you if you do."

He committed her face to memory and answered, "I suspect you won't."

FIFTEEN

"Cole's injured. We can't leave him behind." Sierra jogged across the backyard to keep up with Zach's long strides, lugging the diaper bag with her.

"I hear you." Zach opened the gate for her with one hand while maintaining his grip on Danny's carrier with the other. "Cole wanted us to find a neighbor *behind* Pearl's property," he reminded her.

Sierra rushed through the open gate to the un-developed landscape beyond the wooden fence. "The nearest house is at least a half mile away."

"And there's not enough brush to provide cover." Zach didn't slow for even a second.

Reality dawned on her, and she hurried to reach his side. "Cole plans to shoot it out, so we'll have time to run far away from here, but he sprained his right hand. He's no match for Vogel."

"But I am." Zach guided her toward the next-door neighbor's property by following the fence line. "I'm an expert marksman. I'll find a place up the hill where I can get my sights on the bomber, but not until I hide you and Danny."

She didn't want to be the reason why Zach had to delay saving his brother, but she had to think of her nephew. They stopped at the corner of the fence and scanned their surroundings before running across the open area to the backside of the neighbor's house. There was a shed at the far end of the unenclosed yard. Hiding inside was a last resort; the idea of standing in the dark, without knowing if Vogel was coming for them, made her feel like a sitting duck.

They reached the end of the house, and Zach spied around the corner. "The bomber's still at the top of the hill," he whispered. "I can get off a clean shot from here."

The sliding glass door suddenly opened, and a well-dressed older woman, maybe in her late fifties, stepped out, brandishing a gun. "Get off my property or I'll shoot."

Zach held up his free hand. "Ma'am—"

"We're trying to save a baby," Sierra interjected. "He's my nephew. A murderer carjacked the police cruiser parked in the middle of the street. He's going to kill the detective trying to help us if his brother here can't stop him."

The woman held tight to her weapon, which

looked at odds with her pink cashmere sweater and expertly styled gray hair. "And what's that got to do with the baby?"

"After he kills the detective," Zach continued, "he'll go after Sierra and Danny here. You can call the police and ask to speak to the lieutenant. He'll verify what I'm telling you."

"Zach works with search and rescue," Sierra added.

"I have an official ID card in my wallet," Zach said. "It proves I work with the police department."

The neighbor kept the gun aimed at him. "Get it out—slowly."

He removed his wallet from his back pocket and showed her both his search and rescue ID and his driver's license. "Pearl owns the house next door. You can call her, too. She's my mother's best friend."

Danny started to fuss, and the woman relented. "Don't just stand there. Bring the baby inside."

Zach handed Sierra the carrier. "I'll go after Vogel."

"Be careful." She said a silent prayer for his safety as well as Cole's.

Zach headed back to the corner, crouched and then rushed toward the shed. It was a smart move to draw any possible gunfire away from the house.

Sierra entered the dining room and was greeted by a pumpkin pie aroma flowing from an essential-oil diffuser.

"I already called the police," the woman said, lowering her gun. "I heard the man yelling demands from the squad car, and he didn't sound like a police officer."

"Thank you for helping us," Sierra said, taking in the spotless, modern kitchen. "The police should be here soon. The lieutenant told the detective that backup was only a few miles away."

"Two minutes is up." The loud, angry voice coming from the street, not much farther up the hill, belonged to Vogel.

"He sounds like a horrible man," the woman said with a cringe.

"He's evil." Tears welled in Sierra's eyes, and the woman's expression softened.

"My name's Rita. I'm sorry I was rude before, but it's hard to know who to trust." Danny began to fuss again, and the woman pointed to the living room. "Bring the baby in here, where you can sit and wait for the police to come."

"Thank you so much for taking us in." Sierra wanted to tell Rita how she understood her need to be cautious, but she feared the dam holding back her tears might burst if she said too much.

Instead, she quietly followed the woman into the living room.

"Hold the papers out the window again." Vogel's demands sounded louder coming through the house's large window.

Sierra hesitated, her mind drifting to Cole, wondering if he was complying. She needed a view of the action. After placing the carrier down by the sofa, she unstrapped Danny and pulled him into her arms. He gurgled and kicked with joy, unaware of the danger outside the door.

Rita slipped her gun into a drawer in the corner table, then picked up a framed picture from the table. "This is my daughter and her family. I have five grandchildren," she explained, then smiled softly at Danny. "God's children are precious."

"They are," Sierra agreed, convinced the tough woman was a good person who had simply been surprised and cautious when she spotted them snooping around back. She propped Danny in the corner of the sofa. "Would you mind keeping an eye on him?"

Her eyes sparkled with delight, despite the danger outside. "I'd love to."

Once the woman took her place next to Danny, Sierra rushed over to the window. Hiding behind a sheer curtain, she peered through the glass. No sign of life came from the house directly across the street. Every window blind was shut tight. Uphill, the police cruiser remained parked in the middle of the road, and downhill, at the end of the cul-de-sac, Cole reached out through the open blinds to wave the fake ledger and ID copies.

Vogel anchored his arm on the car's window frame and aimed a gun at Cole.

Two shots rang out, each originating from a different location. One bullet hit the cruiser's side mirror, leaving it hanging. The other struck Vogel's hand, forcing him to drop the gun.

Sierra gasped and jerked back from the window.

"What happened?" the woman demanded to know, placing her body in front of Danny.

"Someone shot the bad guy's hand."

"Heaven help us," the woman prayed. "You should get away from there."

"He can't hurt us now." Sirens broke the silence outside, and Sierra's shoulders relaxed as she turned to Rita. "He dropped the gun out of the car, and help is almost here. If he's smart, he'll drive far away as fast as he can."

To her dismay, instead of making a U-turn, Vogel started moving forward—toward Cole.

"What are you up to now?" Cole mumbled as he watched the cruiser roll down the hill. His last shot had hit the car's side mirror. His aim was close, considering he was using his less dominant hand. This time, he zeroed in on the front tire.

He couldn't see Zach near the neighbor's house but knew the second shot, the one that hit Vogel, must have come from him. His brother's decision to stick around instead of fleeing didn't come as a surprise, but it bothered him just the same. He hoped Sierra and Danny were someplace safe.

"No one will ever see those pages again," Vogel growled over the cruiser's loudspeaker.

Sirens grew louder as their backup approached. Not close enough to help this minute. He figured they were near the high school on the main road.

Cole and Zach blew out the cruiser's tires, but the vehicle continued to descend faster, even as the tread flew off, leaving only the rims. Nothing slowed him down.

"What is he...?" A memory from the meeting with the FBI at the police station hit him hard. Vogel had killed one of his victims with a car bomb he sent down a hill into a house. It blew up on impact.

The thought squeezed his lungs like a vise. Cole couldn't escape in time with a wounded leg. He had to stop the car. Aiming at the engine block, he continued shooting until he ran out of ammo.

The cruiser was now close enough for Cole to see Vogel sitting in the driver's seat. His movements gave the impression he was trying to open the door but couldn't. One shot must have jammed the locking mechanism, and it looked like the brakes weren't working, either. Vogel was trapped inside the car headed straight for Cole. So now they might both die in a fiery blaze if a bomb exploded.

Cole drew in a ragged breath, then said what might be his final prayer: "God, I pray You'll save my life, but I accept Your will even if it means I won't ever walk out of this house. Thank You for Your many blessings, and please grant Sierra and Danny long, happy lives together."

The car was fifty feet away. Defenseless, Cole's eyes widened. Self-preservation instincts forced him to jump off the chair onto his good leg and hop away from the oncoming car. His tight grip on the chair with one hand kept him from falling as he watched Vogel push his head and arms out the car window in an effort to escape. Another shot popped, no doubt coming from Zach.

Vogel jerked as if hit again. Desperate to escape the runaway vehicle, he tried to crawl across the front seat to the other side of the car, knocking the steering wheel with his efforts. Now thirty feet from the front yard, the cruiser swerved away from the house.

All Cole could see was Vogel's hand reaching up toward the passenger-side window as the car drove out of sight. Seconds later, he heard metal crunching. Then the ground shook as an explosion rocked the neighborhood.

Knocked off balance, Cole fell against the chair, the top rail hitting his chest. Ignoring the pain—which was negligible compared to a gunshot wound—he lifted his head in time to witness a line of cruisers driving down the hill toward them. They took turns parking a safe distance away.

Black smoke roiled into the cul-de-sac. From what he could remember about the oversize lot, Vogel must have driven into a large juniper tree between Pearl's house and the neighbor to his left, across the street from where Zach had been hiding.

Sierra called out Cole's name. He turned to see her rushing down the next-door neighbor's front flagstone path. She was safe. *Thank You, Lord.*

Zach appeared from the shadows.

Cole placed his Glock on the windowsill and waved. "I'm fine!"

Sierra ran toward him, but an officer stopped her. She pointed at the house and said something Cole couldn't hear, but she got nowhere. Zach guided her back to the neighbor's front porch, where an older woman stood, holding Danny.

Other officers waved an ambulance closer to Pearl's driveway. More sirens blared as a fire truck descended the hill toward the flames. From what Cole could see, the bomb hadn't done any damage to the next-door neighbor's house thanks to the large lots.

"Thomas! I'm the only one here." He reached into his pocket for the house key Pearl had left in a kitchen drawer and tossed it to Officer Thomas, who had been instrumental in assisting them from the beginning.

With his adrenaline level dropping, Cole eased into the chair. Was Vogel really gone? Were Sierra and Danny truly safe now? He studied the concerned expression on her face through the open window as she stood, watching him from afar. Zach stuck close to her, Danny and the neighbor.

Officer Thomas, who hadn't been injured when his cruiser flipped near the campsite, entered the rental home and did a double take when spotting Cole. "Man, what did you do to yourself?"

Cole couldn't help but chuckle. "I had a little help." His voice turning serious, he asked, "What happened at the cabin?"

"The bomber's friends showed up. They're behind bars but not talking."

"What about the officer who drove the cruiser Vogel carjacked?"

"She's on her way to the hospital with a serious concussion. He pistol-whipped her, but it looks like she'll be okay." Officer Thomas ushered the EMTs into the living room. While they strapped Cole onto the gurney, he added, "Now that these guys are all dead or locked up, you can get a good night's sleep in that hospital bed they're taking you to."

Cole didn't want to sleep. They'd been through so much that he was having trouble convincing himself it was over.

When they reached the ambulance, he discovered two men wearing FBI jackets, showing their credentials to Sierra. They'd take her away now to help them find the missing evidence that would help close their case. Zach was running interference, no doubt making sure these guys were authentic agents.

"I want to speak to Sierra," Cole told the EMTs.

"She can see you in the hospital."

Frustrated, he clenched his teeth. He didn't want to wait. "But—"

"At the hospital," the older EMT repeated in a firm voice.

While they prepared to lift him into the back of the ambulance, Cole huffed and then captured Sierra's gaze. She looked at him warily, and he couldn't help but wonder what she was thinking. The gunshot to his leg had proved his job was dangerous. Once she knew he would be all right, would she run away from him again?

SIXTEEN

"I give up," Sierra told the FBI agents. They had been more than patient while searching for the ledger copies the past two days, but it was no use. She dropped onto her sofa near Danny, who played with his horse teething ring in the travel crib Zach had bought for him. She hadn't seen either Walker brother since Cole went to the hospital, but she couldn't think about that right now. "I'm done. I've looked everywhere."

The taller, more energetic agent dressed in a gray suit ran a hand through his thick, wavy hair. "Short of demolishing the walls, I think you're right."

Her heart skipped a beat. This was the house she grew up in. "You're not seriously considering—"

"No." The other agent—a senior, guessing by his age and calm demeanor—shook his head. "I could tell if your sister had made a hole in the wall to hide the papers."

Sierra blew out an exasperated breath. She was so tired of going over and over the same ground. "Does it really matter if we find that evidence? Vogel and Shaw are both dead."

The first agent looked to the other with a raised eyebrow. When he received a slight shrug in response, he explained, "Vogel's lookouts—"

"The militia guys?" she asked.

"Correct. One of them caved under pressure and told us the whole story. As you know, Wade Devereaux, the former agent who went by the last name of Shaw, hired Vogel to supply a car bomb and teach him how to plant it in a Louisiana judge's car. The judge's husband was behind the plot. She was divorcing him, and he wouldn't get much with the ironclad prenup he'd signed before they married."

"Vogel wouldn't plant the bomb because he considered the judge a *hot target*," Sierra supplied, remembering she'd heard this much of the story already. "He did kill at least four other people. I saw the ledger copies before Megan hid them."

"We need the names listed in that ledger to close all five cases," the senior agent stated.

Sierra was beginning to understand what was at stake. "The FBI wants to arrest everyone who hired Vogel, and the victims' families deserve closure."

He nodded. "But we're not getting anywhere here." The senior agent headed toward the door. "You're safe now. We don't need you to testify against Vogel's accomplices, so we'll head back to Yuma and assist the agents conducting a more extensive search of Vogel's property for the original ledger."

The taller agent handed her a business card. "Please call me if you find the copies or think of anything else that might help."

"I will." Sierra studied the card emblazoned with his name and FBI insignia as they shut the door behind them. She locked up, making a mental note to add another security bolt soon. Not that she expected more trouble—but after recent events, she doubted she'd ever feel safe again.

Turning, she took in the chaos. Throw pillow stuffing, books, broken knickknacks and picture frames, plus hundreds of other miscellaneous items littered the floor. "This place is a disaster area." She'd managed to put some of her belongings away while back at her house, but there was a long way to go before it would ever feel like a home again. "I don't suppose you care about the mess as long as you have that teething ring."

Danny babbled and waved his arm up and down in a cute response.

She smiled. Having her nephew around warmed her heart. "I suspect you'll talk my ear off before long."

After a half hour of cleaning, she heard a rap at the door. Her nerves were so raw she jumped, but she quickly remembered kidnappers and murderers seldom knocked on the door. Nonetheless, she approached with caution.

A glance through the open living room blinds revealed Mrs. Walker, Cole's mother, waiting with a basket in her arms.

Sierra made quick work of opening the door. "What a nice surprise. I didn't expect to see you so soon."

"I hope you don't mind me stopping by." Mrs. Walker handed Sierra the basket as she entered. "I thought you might want some sweets. I made three kinds of cookies, fudge and cashew-chocolate clusters."

"Mind? Not at all." Sierra breathed in the enticing aroma. "Although I may gain twenty pounds if I eat all this."

"I'll help." The woman grinned. "I thought we could share a treat after we get your place back to normal."

We? "You've done so much already. I can't impose."

"I wouldn't dream of letting you tackle this job alone." Mrs. Walker eyed the front rooms with a sweeping look. "Cole told me what you'd be facing here when I stopped by the hospital to see him."

Guilt punched Sierra in the stomach. While she'd been with the agents the past two days, she hadn't asked to go to the hospital. "The chief called the FBI agents with updates on Cole's condition. I don't have a new phone yet."

"He's up and walking around. They'll release him soon." Mrs. Walker made a beeline for Danny and reached into the crib to touch his blond curls. "I'm sure he would love to hear from you."

Sierra's feelings for Cole were so conflicted. She loved him dearly and had wanted nothing more than to run to him before they took him away in the ambulance. But when she'd returned home, reality sank in. She couldn't handle losing another loved one. She'd been through too much. And it wouldn't be right to let Danny grow up thinking of Cole as a father figure when he might one day die in the line of duty. She couldn't even imagine what that might do to a child who'd lost his mother.

"I'm not ready," Sierra reluctantly admitted.

"Maybe later." Cole's mother's tone implied she understood, even if she wished for more.

"I'll put your kind gift in the kitchen." Glad

to change the subject, Sierra added, "Thank you so much for helping me."

"Anytime, dear. You and Danny are like family."

The unspoken comment—that she would have officially been a Walker if she hadn't left Cole—hung in the air between them. Unable to say anything else, Sierra headed to the kitchen.

After they'd made considerable progress in the front rooms, she put a teakettle on the stove and fed Danny at the dining room table.

Mrs. Walker was placing cookies on a napkin when something of interest appeared to catch her attention. She walked to the bookcase and picked up the dome-shaped paperweight, a knowing smile on her face. "I remember when Cole had this made for you. He pressed the flowers himself, wanting each one to be perfect before sealing them inside."

Sierra nodded, feeling like she'd been caught with her hand in the cookie jar. She'd never had the heart to get rid of the heavy acrylic paperweight after they broke up. "Purple pansies always were my favorite flowers."

Mrs. Walker placed the paperweight on the table between them. "It's obvious to me that your feelings for Cole still run deep. I can tell by the way you look at him. And, judging how he hangs on your every word, the feeling is mutual."

"I love him." She hated to burst the woman's hopes. "But he has a dangerous job, and no amount of praying can keep him safe. He was shot in the leg and would have died if the bullet hit an artery."

Cole's mother patted Sierra's arm. "He lived. God answered our prayers."

"But we don't know His will. Next time, Cole might not live. I couldn't bear to lose anyone else I love." The hurt in her heart was too deep to ever heal.

"God doesn't want us to live our lives in fear. If I dwelled on what could happen to my sons in law enforcement, I wouldn't be able to get out of bed in the morning. Instead, I pray and trust God will protect them."

The kind woman was silent until it was clear Sierra was incapable of responding. "But sometimes we do lose people we love dearly, and God is there to help us through our grief. Did you ever think that He might have sent Cole to you all those years ago to help you through the loss of your parents and grandparents, and that he's back now to help you through the loss of your sister?"

Sierra sighed. "I don't know what to think anymore."

"I wish you could see yourself the way I do. You are so much stronger than you were twelve years ago—even stronger than you were last week. Two mad men were after you, but you didn't fall apart."

"I complained, and yelled, and cried."

"And then pulled yourself together and did what it took to keep Danny safe."

Sierra shifted her gaze to her nephew, who still played with the teething ring. "I would do anything for Danny. He's all I have left of Megan."

Cole's mother watched the baby play quietly for a minute before asking, "Sierra, if you could go back in time to when Megan lived here and you both argued constantly, would you have insisted she stay and not move to Yuma if you knew you would lose her this week?"

What a question! "Of course. Megan was my sister. I loved her and would have wanted to spend every minute I could with her, especially if I knew Shaw would take her from us." While watching Mrs. Walker casually take a cookie from the basket, the lesson behind Mrs. Walker's question opened her eyes. "And I love Cole, too—with all my heart. Point taken."

"You should tell him how you feel." Mrs. Walker hugged her before heading home.

Sierra placed the paperweight back on the

bookshelf, thinking she should visit Cole in the hospital tomorrow. Right now, her mind was whirling.

While placing Danny back in the travel crib, she noticed something brown sticking out from beneath the china cabinet. Crouching, she pulled an extension cord out from its hiding place. "How did you get here?"

She was positive she'd left it in the garage, near the Christmas boxes—and the missing glue sticks. "Megan, did you use the extension cord to plug in the glue gun?" Scanning the front rooms, she searched for a place to hide the ledger and ID copies that would be far enough from an electrical outlet to need a cord. Her gaze landed on the playhouse in the backyard, six feet away from the sliding glass door. She'd assumed the police officer who'd inspected it earlier had moved it closer to the house, but it might have been Megan.

A fake clock kept falling off the plastic wall when she and Megan used to pretend to bake cookies inside the small house as children. Cautiously optimistic, Sierra grabbed a screwdriver from a toolbox in the garage, then rushed out back. Flipping the house over as the officer had done when he inspected it, she discovered the clock had remained securely in place. Anticipation rose in her chest.

She used the screwdriver to pry off the clock. It dropped out of her hands, and her eyes grew wide. Megan had folded the papers, tucked them into the round opening and then hot-glued the clock edges before placing it back where it belonged. No one other than Sierra would have suspected a thing.

"So much violence over three pieces of paper." She opened the copies to peruse them. Assured they were the real thing, she suddenly felt vulnerable. Her gaze flicked about, making sure she was alone as she folded the pages and tucked them into her back pocket.

Sierra wasted no time rushing back into her house, where she shoved more diapers, a pacifier and a prepared bottle into Danny's diaper bag. Without a phone, she had no choice but to take the evidence to the chief at the police station. He could keep the pages safe until the FBI collected them. There wasn't much Cole could do from a hospital bed.

"Going somewhere?" Shaw, very much alive, stood inside the frame of her open sliding glass door.

Cole tapped the side of his hospital bed, anxious to be released. No matter how often he tried to focus on the television mounted to the wall, he still couldn't name a single character in the action movie he'd turned on over an hour ago.

"I hear you're about to be released." The chief of police strode into the room, carrying a white paper bag and drink cup from a local hamburger joint. "I also figured you might be tired of hospital food."

"You figured right." Cole inhaled the aroma of french fries, then released his breath. "You may have just saved my sanity." He eagerly accepted the gift. "Want some?"

"I already ate." The chief looked around the sterile environment. "When's the doctor signing your discharge papers?"

"Any minute now, which is a day later than I wanted."

"Ready to get back to work? Or ready to see a little lady?"

Cole rubbed his chin, not sure he should admit the truth but did anyway. "Both."

"Understandable. The reason I'm here is I have news—quite a bit, in fact."

"About the case?"

"Let's start there. I spoke to the FBI special agent in charge of the case in Louisiana. It turns out Shaw had friends in the agency who didn't know he'd gone bad. One of whom works in the Phoenix field office. His buddy kept him in the loop. Shaw knew which agents headed to Sedona and when they would arrive. Vogel was telling the truth when he claimed Shaw was behind the bombings aimed at the agents and probably the one in the biker bar, too."

Cole remembered the conversation Megan had overheard back in Yuma. "Vogel taught him how to put a bomb together and plant it."

"Exactly." The chief chose a cushioned seat near the window. "Bomb fragments from each explosion and DNA remains are being examined for more information."

"Tying up loose ends," Cole surmised.

"Speaking of which, I've been meaning to tell you I had already decided on the lead detective position before any of this happened."

"Oh?" This couldn't be good. Cole had been relegated to second-rate cases when the lieutenant was fast-tracking Detective Gold. He'd hate for that to be permanent.

"The position's yours if you want it. We gave Detective Gold the chance to prove his worth, but I still prefer your methods and temperament. Not to mention, you know this city inside and out. The past few days confirmed I made the right choice. Gold will be out for a while, but when he's back, I'm sure you two will work well together under your leadership."

Cole couldn't believe his ears. "Thank you for your confidence in me, sir."

He should have jumped at the opportunity to tell the chief he'd take the position, but he hesitated. For the third time, Cole had to choose between his calling and the woman he loved. It felt like torture—or a test. *God, in my heart, I know I'm supposed to work in law enforcement, but I have a hard time accepting that You would send Sierra back into my life if we weren't meant to be together. Please give me Your guidance.*

The door edged open, and the doctor stepped inside. They spent the next few minutes discussing what Cole could and could not do once he left the hospital.

After the doc left the room, the chief filled Cole in on everything else he'd learned from the Louisiana agent. Less than an hour later, they were on their way to Sierra's house to share the fantastic news.

The chief slowed his white Cadillac as they approached the ranch-style house Cole had visited hundreds of times during his early twenties. He should have been excited to see Sierra again, but something didn't feel right.

His gaze traveled from Sierra's SUV parked in the driveway to the front window. He blinked when he spotted her standing there, a look of panic on her face. Her eyes widened as she spotted him in the car.

Sierra mouthed, *Help me*, while twisting the

rod that closed the blinds. She disappeared from view as if gone forever.

Terror shot through his body. "Sierra's in trouble. Park in front of the neighbor's house."

The chief stopped on the curb across from the Anderson family's front door and reached for his phone. "If the nanny cam we hijacked is still working, we can get a front-row seat to what's happening in there."

In less than a minute, they were viewing the footage from the bear Vogel had brought to the house. The feed had been redirected to the station, and the chief knew the password. Sierra stepped into view on the phone's small screen, and Cole's heart squeezed. She glanced up at the bear as if hoping they could see her.

"Move away from the door," a man growled.

Cole recognized the voice, even with the deeper Louisiana accent. Disbelief and terror vied for dominance over his emotions. "Shaw's alive."

The chief's jaw dropped open, but he quickly recovered and called for backup. He then pushed his car door open and ordered, "You stay here."

There was no way Cole would stay put when Sierra's and Danny's lives were in danger. "Chief, I have an idea on how to lure Shaw into the backyard. This neighbor isn't home, but he told me he wants to help. There's a front door key under the ceramic turtle. You can sneak quietly through the house to the backyard, where they have a stack of firewood. If you throw pieces, you can grab Shaw's attention."

"Watch her front door," the chief said before heading toward the Anderson home.

Cole noticed the earbuds in the Cadillac's cup holder. He plugged them into the phone the chief had left behind so he could listen to Shaw and Sierra without attracting attention.

With the phone tucked into his jacket pocket, he hobbled out of the vehicle. Balancing on his good leg, he reached through the back seat's open window for his crutches.

"I don't understand." Sierra's voice quivered as it carried over the airways into his ear. "I saw your boot on the news after the car explosion."

Shaw laughed. "I knew one of you would recognize the paint spot. Both you and that detective are too smart for your own good."

"You faked your death," Sierra stated with incredulous contempt. "Vogel had nothing to do with the explosion."

"Oh, yes, he did. He planted the bomb. Only I wasn't stupid enough to get into a car without inspecting it first—at least, not after our falling out. All this time, I thought he was a psychopath. He cared more about that kid of his than I thought he would."

"A psychopath like you?"

Shaw's grisly chuckle made Cole cringe. He pushed harder against the crutches to move faster across the Anderson's front yard, then Sierra's. He gently tried the front door. Locked.

"Honey," Shaw growled. "I'm not crazy, just greedy."

"Who died in your place?" she asked. "And how did you manage that?"

"Vogel figured out where I was staying. When I found the bomb under the front seat of the car I stole, I left the door open and took off. The motel was in a crime-infested neighborhood. My best guess is a car thief drove it away from the motel and *kablooey*."

Cole hoped Sierra could keep the conversation going. He leaned his left crutch against the front of the house to remove his Glock from the holster. With his weight on his right leg, he risked peering in through a slit in the blinds. Sierra stood in front of the living room bookshelf near the acrylic paperweight he'd given her a decade ago. His heart clenched. He knew she still loved him every bit as much as he loved her.

Shaw stood in front of the dining room table. He must have entered through the open sliding glass door. "Since you haven't found the papers yet, there's no point in delaying—"

"I found them," Sierra blurted out. "I mean, I know where Megan hid them."

A piece of firewood smacked against the plastic house in the backyard.

"What the..." Shaw edged closer to the sliding glass door but didn't go outside.

The crutch leaning against the front of the house fell against a rock with a thwack. Cole jerked back to the safety of the outside wall.

"Who's out there?" Shaw barked.

A bullet splintered the window beside Cole. Pieces of glass fell to the red dirt below.

Cole held his breath. There was nowhere to hide, and Danny's screams were bound to bring Shaw's anger down on him.

Pounding noises came from the backyard. The chief had to be throwing firewood at anything he could find.

With no time to waste, Cole grabbed his Glock, shifted and—despite the pain—peered through the big hole in the window and aimed. "Police!"

Shaw faced the sliding glass door but swung his Beretta back toward the front of the house.

Cole pulled the trigger. His bullet hit Shaw's arm, and his weapon skidded across the dining room tile. Relieved he'd hit his target, Cole yelled, "Hands in the air."

Shaw did his best to comply, blood dripping to the floor. "You shot me!"

Sierra stood frozen in place. She should have run out the front door, but she would never leave her nephew behind. Cole desperately wanted to rush in and grab her, but he didn't dare take his eyes or gun off Shaw for even a second.

The chief appeared at the back sliding glass door and entered with his pistol aimed at Shaw. He was handcuffing the former FBI agent when sirens split the air and cruisers swarmed the front curb. Officer Thomas was the first to exit his vehicle.

With Shaw now in cuffs, Sierra ran to her crying nephew and scooped him out of the travel crib before leaving the house. Out front, Officer Thomas led her away toward a cruiser. She turned as they left the front yard. "Cole!"

"I'm coming." He holstered his Glock and told the officers the suspect had been apprehended, then used the crutch he leaned on to reach for the one that had fallen against the rock.

Shaw appeared on the front porch, his hands handcuffed behind his back and the chief holding a pistol to him. The prisoner sneered at Cole. "I should have killed you when I had the chance."

"I guess you should've." He turned to find

Officer Thomas, holding Danny, and Sierra running his way.

Cole held his hands out for her, wishing he wasn't leaning on crutches.

She rushed into his arms and buried her face in his shoulder. "I was so afraid he'd kill you."

"Don't you know by now that I'm made of Kevlar?" He smoothed her silky blond hair with his good hand, his right wrist stinging from shooting with a heavy gun.

"Not funny." She pulled back enough to meet his gaze, her blue eyes wet with unshed tears. "I've been such a fool. We could have been so happy together these past twelve years. I love you and want to be with you—no matter how long we have left on this earth."

"I love you, too, more than you'll ever know. Are you sure you can handle dating a detective?" He'd tell her about his promotion later.

"I'm more than sure. I'm positive. A man shot at you, and I'm not running for the hills."

He reached out for her hand. "Let's go inside. I have some news for you."

"I do, too. I found the ledger copies in the playhouse." She removed them from her back pocket.

Cole had trouble believing the evidence had finally been found. "The FBI will be glad to see these."

"Now, what did you want to tell me?" Sierra studied him. "I am so much stronger than I was when this all started. Whatever you have to say, you can tell me here and now. I don't want to wait."

"Okay." He drew in a deep breath, wondering how to break the news to her. Deciding the direct approach would be best, he said, "Megan's alive."

EPILOGUE

Six months later, Sierra removed a baking sheet from the oven and placed it on the stove. The aroma of peanut butter cookies wafted into the air.

"Something smells good in there." Cole's voice carried in from the living room, where he was playing with Danny. He'd been over almost every day since her nightmare had ended.

News of Megan's death had been a case of mistaken identity. An inexperienced online reporter had heard that a woman who had been held captive in a rental property was rushed to the hospital. Inside the emergency room, a different woman died, and the reporter jumped to the wrong conclusion.

The agent in charge of the FBI in New Orleans decided it was in Megan's best interest not to correct the internet reports of her death. And with a suspected leak somewhere in law enforcement, they decided to keep her in a safe house until the time was right to reveal the truth. With a concussion, she couldn't remember where she'd hid the ledger and ID copies, only that they were at the house.

The evidence, once found, sealed Shaw's fate. As a condition of his plea bargain, he confessed to planting the car bomb that had killed the Louisiana judge and named her husband as the man who'd hired him to do the job.

"Save some of those cookies for me." The sound of Megan's voice brought joy to Sierra's soul.

"I made enough for all of us." She stepped into the living room, where Megan sat on the sofa, compiling Sierra's landscape photos into a coffee table book.

Megan had turned over a new leaf after this ordeal. She took over the marketing and bookkeeping end of the photography business while staying home with Danny. This arrangement freed Sierra to book more photo shoots.

"Yum, cookies," Cole told Danny. They sat on the living room area rug, playing with blocks. The baby was nine months old now and could sit up by himself. He could also crawl and walk if he held on to the sofa or coffee table for support.

Danny waved his arms and tossed a white block.

Wait a minute. That's not a block. Sierra stepped closer, studying the shape of the object. "Does he have a jewelry box?"

Cole scratched his chin. "I don't know. Maybe you should check."

Megan lifted her phone and, wearing a huge grin, began to record a video.

Sierra's gaze traveled between Cole and her sister. She tried not to guess what they were up to, not wanting her hopes to be dashed.

She walked over and picked up the box. When she pulled the top back, her heart exploded. Inside was a sparkling diamond. At least two karats.

Her breath caught in her throat.

Cole pushed up to one knee. "Sierra Lowery, would you do me the honor of being my wife?" When Danny crawled closer, Cole lifted him onto his knee. "Your nephew thinks you should."

Tears welled in Sierra's eyes. One day, they would have children who would ride horses on the ranch alongside Danny. "Yes." She dropped to her knees and kissed him. "I will marry you, Cole Walker, for better or worse, for the rest of our lives."

* * * * *

Dear Reader:

I hope you enjoyed this trip back to Walker Ranch outside Sedona. In this follow-up to *Ranch Under Fire*, God sent Cole into Sierra's life to help her through the loss of her grandmother and parents, then again when she needed to protect her nephew. In my own life, He sent a new friend and compassionate adults to help me through a total upheaval during my teen years. I didn't recognize His gift until many years later. Sierra didn't either until Cole's mother pointed it out to her. I take great comfort in knowing we are never totally alone; God is always with us.

I love to connect with readers. My newsletter subscribers receive behind-the-scenes updates on my books. I hope you'll join us through my website at authortinawheeler.com.

Blessings,
Tina

Get 3 FREE REWARDS!

We'll send you 2 FREE Books plus a FREE Mystery Gift.

FREE
Value Over
$20

Both the **Harlequin® Special Edition** and **Harlequin® Heartwarming™** series feature compelling novels filled with stories of love and strength where the bonds of friendship, family and community unite.

YES! Please send me 2 FREE novels from the Harlequin Special Edition or Harlequin Heartwarming series and my FREE Gift (gift is worth about $10 retail). After receiving them, if I don't wish to receive any more books, I can return the shipping statement marked "cancel." If I don't cancel, I will receive 6 brand-new Harlequin Special Edition books every month and be billed just $5.49 each in the U.S. or $6.24 each in Canada, a savings of at least 12% off the cover price, or 4 brand-new Harlequin Heartwarming Larger-Print books every month and be billed just $6.24 each in the U.S. or $6.74 each in Canada, a savings of at least 19% off the cover price. It's quite a bargain! Shipping and handling is just 50¢ per book in the U.S. and $1.25 per book in Canada.* I understand that accepting the 2 free books and gift places me under no obligation to buy anything. I can always return a shipment and cancel at any time by calling the number below. The free books and gift are mine to keep no matter what I decide.

Choose one: ☐ **Harlequin Special Edition** (235/335 BPA GRMK)   ☐ **Harlequin Heartwarming Larger-Print** (161/361 BPA GRMK)   ☐ **Or Try Both!** (235/335 & 161/361 BPA GRPZ)

Name (please print)

Address   Apt. #

City   State/Province   Zip/Postal Code

Email: Please check this box ☐ if you would like to receive newsletters and promotional emails from Harlequin Enterprises ULC and its affiliates. You can unsubscribe anytime.

Mail to the **Harlequin Reader Service:**
IN U.S.A.: P.O. Box 1341, Buffalo, NY 14240-8531
IN CANADA: P.O. Box 603, Fort Erie, Ontario L2A 5X3

Want to try 2 free books from another series? Call 1-800-873-8635 or visit www.ReaderService.com.

*Terms and prices subject to change without notice. Prices do not include sales taxes, which will be charged (if applicable) based on your state or country of residence. Canadian residents will be charged applicable taxes. Offer not valid in Quebec. This offer is limited to one order per household. Books received may not be as shown. Not valid for current subscribers to the Harlequin Special Edition or Harlequin Heartwarming series. All orders subject to approval. Credit or debit balances in a customer's account(s) may be offset by any other outstanding balance owed by or to the customer. Please allow 4 to 6 weeks for delivery. Offer available while quantities last.

Your Privacy—Your information is being collected by Harlequin Enterprises ULC, operating as Harlequin Reader Service. For a complete summary of the information we collect, how we use this information and to whom it is disclosed, please visit our privacy notice located at corporate.harlequin.com/privacy-notice. From time to time we may also exchange your personal information with reputable third parties. If you wish to opt out of this sharing of your personal information, please visit readerservice.com/consumerschoice or call 1-800-873-8635. **Notice to California Residents**—Under California law, you have specific rights to control and access your data. For more information on these rights and how to exercise them, visit corporate.harlequin.com/california-privacy.

HSEHW23

Get 3 FREE REWARDS!

We'll send you 2 FREE Books plus a FREE Mystery Gift.

FREE
Value Over
$20

Both the **Mystery Library** and **Essential Suspense** series feature compelling novels filled with gripping mysteries, edge-of-your-seat thrillers and heart-stopping romantic suspense stories.

YES! Please send me 2 FREE novels from the Mystery Library or Essential Suspense Collection and my FREE Gift (gift is worth about $10 retail). After receiving them, if I don't wish to receive any more books, I can return the shipping statement marked "cancel." If I don't cancel, I will receive 4 brand-new Mystery Library books every month and be billed just $6.74 each in the U.S. or $7.24 each in Canada, a savings of at least 25% off the cover price, or 4 brand-new Essential Suspense books every month and be billed just $7.49 each in the U.S. or $7.74 each in Canada, a savings of at least 17% off the cover price. It's quite a bargain! Shipping and handling is just 50¢ per book in the U.S. and $1.25 per book in Canada.* I understand that accepting the 2 free books and gift places me under no obligation to buy anything. I can always return a shipment and cancel at any time by calling the number below. The free books and gift are mine to keep no matter what I decide.

Choose one: ☐ **Mystery Library**   ☐ **Essential**   ☐ **Or Try Both!**
　　　　　　　　(414/424 BPA GRPM)　　**Suspense**　　　(414/424 & 191/391
　　　　　　　　　　　　　　　　　　　(191/391 BPA GRPM)　　BPA GRRZ)

Name (please print)

Address   Apt. #

City   State/Province   Zip/Postal Code

Email: Please check this box ☐ if you would like to receive newsletters and promotional emails from Harlequin Enterprises ULC and its affiliates. You can unsubscribe anytime.

Mail to the Harlequin Reader Service:
IN U.S.A.: P.O. Box 1341, Buffalo, NY 14240-8531
IN CANADA: P.O. Box 603, Fort Erie, Ontario L2A 5X3

Want to try 2 free books from another series? Call 1-800-873-8635 or visit www.ReaderService.com.

---

*Terms and prices subject to change without notice. Prices do not include sales taxes, which will be charged (if applicable) based on your state or country of residence. Canadian residents will be charged applicable taxes. Offer not valid in Quebec. This offer is limited to one order per household. Books received may not be as shown. Not valid for current subscribers to the Mystery Library or Essential Suspense Collection. All orders subject to approval. Credit or debit balances in a customer's account(s) may be offset by any other outstanding balance owed by or to the customer. Please allow 4 to 6 weeks for delivery. Offer available while quantities last.

Your Privacy—Your information is being collected by Harlequin Enterprises ULC, operating as Harlequin Reader Service. For a complete summary of the information we collect, how we use this information and to whom it is disclosed, please visit our privacy notice located at corporate.harlequin.com/privacy-notice. From time to time we may also exchange your personal information with reputable third parties. If you wish to opt out of this sharing of your personal information, please visit readerservice.com/consumerschoice or call 1-800-873-8635. **Notice to California Residents**—Under California law, you have specific rights to control and access your data. For more information on these rights and how to exercise them, visit corporate.harlequin.com/california-privacy.

MYSSTS23

HARLEQUIN
PLUS

Try the best multimedia subscription service for romance readers like you!

Read, Watch and Play.

Experience the easiest way to get the romance content you crave.

Start your **FREE TRIAL** at
<u>www.harlequinplus.com/freetrial</u>.